Penguin Book 2370

Wonderful Clouds

Françoise Sagan was born in 1935. Her father is a
prosperous Paris industrialist whose family were
originally Spanish. She took her *nom de plume* from the
Princesse de Sagan of Marcel Proust. She was eighteen
years old when she wrote her best-selling *Bonjour
Tristesse*. She had failed to pass her examinations at the
Sorbonne and she decided to write a novel. The book
received great acclaim in France, where in 1959 it had
sold 850,000 copies, and also abroad. Her second and
third books, *A Certain Smile* and *Those Without Shadows*,
have also had tremendous popularity in France, Great
Britain, and the U.S.A. Her fourth book, *Aimez-vous
Brahms* . . ., appeared in 1959. All these books have been
published in Penguins. She has also written four plays, and
her most recent novel is *La Chamade*.

Her hobby is driving fast cars, of which she has five,
and in 1957 she was involved in a bad road accident.
Her ballet *The Broken Date* has been produced in Paris
and London.

Françoise Sagan

Wonderful Clouds

Translated by Anne Green

Penguin Books

Penguin Books Ltd, Harmondsworth, Middlesex, England
Penguin Books Australia Ltd, Ringwood, Victoria, Australia

Les Merveilleux Nuages first published 1961
This translation published by John Murray 1961
Published in Penguin Books 1965
Reprinted 1968

Made and printed in Great Britain by
Cox & Wyman Ltd, London, Reading and Fakenham
Set in Monotype Baskerville

à mon ami Philippe

L'étranger

– Qui aimes-tu le mieux, homme énigmatique, dis?
Ton père, ta mère, ta sœur, ou ton frère?
– Je n'ai ni père, ni mère, ni sœur, ni frère.
– Tes amis?
– Vous vous servez là d'une parole dont le sens m'est
resté jusqu'à ce jour inconnu.
– Ta patrie?
– J'ignore sous quelle latitude elle est située.
– La beauté?
– Je l'aimerais volontiers déesse et immortelle.
– L'or?
– Je le hais comme vous haïssez Dieu.
– Eh! Qu'aimes-tu donc, extraordinaire étranger?
– J'aime les nuages . . . les nuages qui passent . . . là-bas
. . . là-bas . . . les merveilleux nuages!

CHARLES BAUDELAIRE
(*Poèmes en prose*)

Florida

I

The mangrove stood out black against Key Largo's garish
blue sky and its formal, dried-up shape seemed less like a
tree than some sinister insect. Josée closed her eyes, sighing. Real trees were a long way away at present, especially
the poplar of her childhood days, the poplar that stood by
itself in a corner of the field near the house. She used to lie
under it, her feet propped against the trunk, watching
hundreds of little leaves shaken by the wind, all bending
the same way, and, high, high in the air, the distant height
of the slender tree top, so fine that it seemed about to take
flight. How old could she have been then, fourteen, fifteen?
Or else she would lean against the trunk, her head in her
hands, her mouth pressed close to the rough bark, whispering promises to herself, drawing in her own breath, disturbed by adolescence, by terror of the future and by its
very inevitability. She never imagined that she would
leave her poplar, or that returning ten years later, she
would find it cut to the ground, the scars of the axe on the
trunk hard and dry.

'What are you thinking about?'

'About a tree.'

'What tree?'

'A tree you don't know,' she said, and began laughing.

'Of course.'

Without opening her eyes she felt the mounting tension
that she always did when Alan's voice took on a certain
tone.

'I'm thinking of a poplar, when I was eight.'

Then she wondered why she had put her age back in telling him about it. Perhaps because she imagined that by moving farther away in time, Alan's jealousy would cool slightly. No, at eight years old, he would not ask, 'Who were you in love with?'

There was a pause, but he was aroused, she could sense him thinking at her side, and his torpor of a moment ago had given way to intense interest. She could also feel the canvas of the deck-chair against her back and a drop of sweat at the nape of her neck running on and on.

'Why did you marry me?' he asked.

'Because I loved you.'

'And now?'

'I still love you.'

'Why?'

That was the way it began. These three questions were like the three classic knocks before the curtain goes up in a French theatre: a sort of convention which they had come tacitly to accept, before Alan proceeded to tear himself to pieces.

'Not now, Alan,' she implored.

'What made you love me?'

'I took you for a very quiet American – I've told you this a hundred times over – and I thought you very attractive.'

'And now?'

'I take you for an unquiet American and you're as attractive as ever.'

'An American full of neuroses? With a mother who has too much money . . .'

'Yes, all right, so I did marry the image I formed of you, is that what you want me to say?'

'I want you to love me.'

'I do love you.'

'No.'

'How I wish the others would come back,' she thought,

8

'and come back quickly. What an idea to go fishing in this heat! He'll drink a little too much, he'll drive too fast, he'll sleep like a log. He'll sleep so close to me that he'll crush me, and I'll find myself loving him for an hour or so because he seems so lost. Tomorrow morning, he'll tell me about all the horrible dreams he's had. He has an extraordinary imagination.'

She sat up and looked at the white jetty. Not a soul in sight. She relaxed in her chair.

'No sign of them yet,' he said acidly, 'too bad. You're bored, aren't you?'

She turned her head towards him. He was staring at her. He was really too much like the young hero of a Western: china blue eyes, bronzed skin, frank expression. Simplicity itself, apparently. Alan. Yes, she had loved him and still loved him a little when she looked at him closely. But more and more often lately, she looked away.

'Well? Shall we go on?'

'If you must.'

'How did you feel when I asked you to marry me?'

'I felt happy.'

'Is that all?'

'I had the impression of being rescued. I . . . I was worn out, you know that perfectly well.'

'Worn out . . . Who by?'

'By Europe.'

'Who in Europe?'

'I've told you about it.'

'Tell me again.'

'I'll go away,' thought Josée suddenly. 'I must be quite clear, I must get that firmly into my head. I'll go away. He can do whatever he likes, commit suicide if he must, he's talked about it often enough. That phoney psychiatrist of his has talked about it often enough too. So has his mother. All right, let him kill himself. Let him go mad like

9

his wretched father. Let them all get on with their stupid drunken lives. *Vive la France* and Benjamin Constant!'

Yet at the same time, it filled her with nausea to think of Alan as dead, Alan who was so haunted by death. 'The first excuse that comes along will be the right one and I don't want to be that excuse.'

'That's blackmail,' she said.

'So what? I know what you're thinking about.'

'I can't have any respect for you so long as you try that kind of blackmail on me,' she said weakly.

'Why should that worry me?'

'Why indeed?'

What did he care about her respect? Besides, the low opinion she had of herself tended to be catching. She was reduced to playing the part of a life-line, a safety device against disaster. At twenty-seven. Only three years ago, in Paris, living alone or with whomever she pleased, she could breathe freely. Now, she was perspiring in this artificial setting with a neurotic young husband who had no idea what he expected of her. She began to laugh and he sat upright, eyes screwed up. He hated her to laugh on such occasions, although sometimes he had a sense of humour.

'Stop laughing like that.'

But she went on laughing softly and with a kind of tenderness as she thought of her apartment in Paris, of the streets at night, of the wild, carefree years. Alan got up.

'Aren't you thirsty? You'll get sunstroke, darling. Would you like me to fetch you some orange juice?'

He knelt, laid his head on her arm, looked up at her. That was his second weapon: whenever she escaped his jealousy, he grew affectionate. She ran her hand over his even features, outlined with her fingers the firm mouth and wide set eyes, wondering yet again what made the quiet virility of his face so ineffectual.

'I'd rather you brought me a Bacardi,' she said.

10

He smiled. He liked drinking and liked her to drink with him. She had been warned against that too. But although she was not particularly fond of alcohol, there were times when she felt like getting drunk and remaining so for the rest of her life.

'Two Bacardis, then,' he said.

He kissed her hand. A white-haired woman in flowered shorts threw them a tender, approving glance, but Josée did not smile back. Her eyes followed Alan as he walked gracefully away with the confident stride of someone for whom life has always been too easy, and, as happened each time that he went away, a feeling of sadness overcame her. 'Yet I don't love him any longer,' she whispered and quickly shielded her face with her arm, as though the sun itself might contradict her.

*

When the others returned, they found them lying on the sand, Josée's head on Alan's shoulder, talking passionately about books. Several glasses were scattered around, and Brandon Kinnel's glance mutely pointed these out to his wife. Eve Kinnel was both intelligent and ugly, but not aggressively so. She was fond of Josée and, like Brandon, apprehensive of Alan. Indeed, the Kinnels saw eye to eye about everything, shared everything except, of course, Brandon's hopeless and secret infatuation for Josée.

'What a day!' cried Eve. 'Three hours at sea for one miserable barracuda . . .'

'Why range the seas?' asked Alan. 'Happiness is right here on the beach.'

He kissed Josée's hair. She looked up, saw Brandon's eyes resting on the empty glasses and mentally sent him to hell. She had whiled away a pleasant hour. She felt happy, the landscape was superb, Alan brilliant and relaxed: did it matter if a few Bacardis had contributed to this? She laid her hand on Alan's bronzed leg.

'Happiness is right here on the beach,' she repeated.

Brandon looked away. 'I've hurt his feelings,' she thought, 'I suppose he must be in love with me. Funny, I've never thought of it.' She held out her hand to him:

'Help me up, Brandon, the sun's made me dizzy.'

She stressed the word 'sun'. He stretched out his hand. A good many people wondered why Brandon Kinnel, who looked like an absent-minded buccaneer, had come to marry Eve who looked like an ant. There were two reasons why he had: she was understanding and he, timid. So he helped Josée up and she staggered and clung to him.

'What about me, Eve,' Alan complained, 'are you going to leave me here on the beach, all alone, all night? You can see for yourself that I'm as drunk as Josée, because she's drunk too. She told you we were happy, didn't she?'

He lay on the sand, gazing up at them with a little smile. Josée dropped Brandon's arm and then grasped it firmly again.

'If you can't stand a couple of drinks, that's your affair, *I'm* dead sober and, what's more, I'm hungry. I'll have dinner with Brandon.'

She wheeled around, forgetting Eve. For the first time for a year she remembered that there were other men in the world beside Alan.

'He's too tactless,' she thought aloud. 'He ruins everything.'

'You ought to leave him,' said Brandon.

'He'd be a wreck, that is, I mean . . .'

'He's a wreck already.'

'I know.'

'But an attractive one, isn't that it?'

She opened her mouth to protest, then shrugged her shoulders.

'Yes, that's probably it.'

They walked slowly towards the restaurant. Brandon

could feel Josée's hand on his arm and wondered if he should not withdraw it before they reached the restaurant. His arm had got into an awkward position and a sort of cramp paralysed it.

'I hate you to drink,' he said.

He spoke too loudly, too emphatically and knew it. Josée raised her head.

'Alan's mother hates it too. So do I. But what can it matter to you?'

He freed his arm, mildly relieved. This was one of the rare occasions he had ever talked to her alone and he had managed to irritate her.

'No, it's none of my business.'

She turned and looked at him as he was walking at her side, with his arms dangling. He had a straightforward reassuring face. She imagined when she married him that Alan was this sort of man.

'You're right, Brandon. Forgive me. Your arguments are so practical, which is not always a European virtue. I live with Alan, you see. I can't tell myself "I must leave him," as I might say, "I must have my appendix out."'

'Yet you must, Josée, and if there's anything I can do to help . . .'

'Thank you, Brandon. I know. You and Eve are very kind.'

'Not only Eve and me, I meant just me.'

He was scarlet. Josée did not answer. Yet, in Paris, she used to enjoy teasing men and would have seized on an opportunity like this. 'I've grown older,' she thought. The restaurant was full. In the distance on the beach, the shadowy forms of Eve and Alan followed slowly behind them.

*

Once more they were alone and at home. The bungalow consisted of three very long rooms, furnished in light coloured bamboo, decorated with Negro masks, curious objects of plaited straw, harpoons, anything and everything that satisfied Alan's mother's idea of what was exotic. Although Alan had lived there alone for a long time, there was no hint of his presence. The books and records they had brought together from New York. She had never known a man so little interested in his own past. He could only see himself in his relation to her, in which he adopted so sedulously the role of tormentor that she sometimes wanted to laugh. In fact, he shaped their relationship into such a set pattern and abandoned himself so completely to it that she was occasionally seized with a kind of dizziness, like when she saw a bad play or a pretentious film. But in this case the ambitious author of the bad play, or of the pretentious film, was Alan, and she could only wait for the unavoidable flop and grieve with him.

He was pacing up and down before her. All the windows were open and the warm Florida air lightly touched their cheeks, bringing with it the smell of the sea, of exhaust fumes and perpetual heat. She watched him as he moved to and fro, thinking that she had never felt so alienated from her surroundings or from her life. And had never been so sensitive – so exposed – to anyone.

'Brandon's in love with you,' he said finally.

She smiled. He always noticed everything precisely when she did. Two days earlier, she would have taxed him with being obsessed. Two days later, with being blind. Yet she knew that she could not joke with him over such things as she might with any other man.

'What has Brandon got?' he asked dreamily, and stopped walking to lean against a window.

'Nothing much,' she answered.

'Let's see . . .' he continued. 'He's a fine figure of a man, solid, reassuring. The only possible man in Key Largo at present. His wife is intelligent and knows how to behave herself. I can very well imagine his knocking me down if I insulted you. You know, the perfect gentleman: "There are things, old boy, that a man can't put up with and Lady Josée's above suspicion . . . etc." '

He began to laugh.

'You don't say anything. Do you think such a scene unlikely?'

'No. Nothing seems unlikely to me.'

'Even sleeping with him?'

'No. But it doesn't appeal to me very much either.'

'Oh, but it will, in time. You'll see.'

He moved away from the window, and once again she was struck by his sense of theatre. He liked to adopt an attitude before speaking his lines, and he calculated his silences with almost professional care, as though he felt the need of underlining what he had to say by appropriate 'business'. She watched him through half-closed eyes, lying on a canvas chaise-longue with her hands clasped behind her head. She felt sleepy and yet could not help wondering how much longer she would be able to bear all this. She smiled to herself. Today for the first time she had formulated her feelings in definite terms: 'I've got to get out of here.'

'Maybe Brandon bores you to death, but you shouldn't make such a secret of it,' continued Alan. 'You whisked him off the beach in fine style, leaving poor Eve alone with me. She looked wretched as she watched you two go off.'

'That didn't cross my mind. Do you think . . .'

She was about to ask, 'Do you think I've hurt her feelings?' but stopped. In any case, he was bound to answer, 'Yes.' He always tried to create a sense of guilt in her. Suddenly she felt furious.

'I didn't hurt her feelings. Eve trusts me. So does Brandon. *They* don't imagine that I live on my back, arms outstretched, waiting for a male. They're normal.'

'Meaning that I'm not?'

'You know perfectly well you're not and you're proud of it, aren't you? You cosset your little neuroses from morning to night. You'd be desperate if you had to come down to earth and behave like an ordinary human being . . .'

'My God,' she thought as she said this, 'I'm talking like the *Reader's Digest*. Me of all people, who loathe common sense, I'm preaching at him like a heavy uncle. In the end he'll succeed in turning me into a bore. And he'll be delighted.'

And sure enough, he came up to her, smiling.

'Josée, do you remember what you told me once: "People have to be accepted as they are, I've never wanted to change anyone, no one has the right to say a word about anyone else." Remember?'

He sat by her, talking so gently that she could no longer be sure whether he was repeating her words like a sort of gospel on which his happiness depended, or whether he simply wanted to shame her. Yes, she had said that, one winter day in New York. They had spent an hour with Alan's mother, and she had left with him afterwards, full of tenderness, compassion and fine principles. They had walked for an hour in Central Park, and he had seemed so bewildered, so dependent on her . . .

'Yes, I did say it. And thought it. And still think it.' She paused, then went on more softly: 'Alan, you aren't helping me.'

'You think I'm being deliberately cruel?'

'Yes.'

And she shut her eyes. He had won by making her admit that he caused her pain, which was exactly what he wanted: to pierce her defences, to hurt her deeply, no matter how. He took her in his arms, raised her up, then laid her down by him, his head on her shoulder. Whispering her name beseechingly, caressing her. He would have liked her to cry. But she didn't cry. Then he made love to her, just as she was, half dressed, and all but grudged her the pleasure which they shared. Later, he undressed her and carried her to their bedroom, asleep. And there, he fell asleep himself, clutching her hand tightly. In the morning she found him still sprawled out across the bed: he had fallen asleep before he could get into it.

'A strange portrait of a sleeper . . . One hand lying open on the sheet, face turned away, legs pulled up against his chest. There was a name for that, what was it? The foetus position. Did Alan miss his mother, his unbearable mother? Had Freud foreseen Alan's mother?' She began to laugh and reached out for a glass of water. 'I hate Bacardi. I hate this tasteless, sterilized water as it runs down my throat. I hate this closed window and this air-conditioning. I hate bamboo and two-dollar African mascots. I hate travelling and tropical landscapes. Do I hate this stranger sprawled out asleep across my bed?

'He is very beautiful. His thighs are long and smooth, the slender thighs of a youth, thighs so smooth to the touch of my lips. I can't hate this young man. I turn my head a little and the stranger sighs, stirs when my mouth touches his skin, before awaking completely. But now it isn't because he's being torn from sleep, he is sighing from enjoyment. His legs outstretched, he has left his mother, found his mistress once more. *Mère des souvenirs, maîtresse des maîtresses* . . . Baudelaire? Verlaine? I shall never know which. He has taken me by the back of the neck, turned me over, drawn me gently to him. He whispers my name: it's true that I'm called Josée and he, Alan. It's impossible that all this should mean nothing, Alan, it's impossible that things should ever be the same again after this, it's impossible that I could ever want to say any name but yours.'

'You've forgotten your hat.'

He shrugged his shoulders. The car was already whirring or rather, purring. It was an old dark red Chevrolet. Alan took no interest in sports cars.

'It's going to be terribly hot,' insisted Josée.

'Get in. Brandon will lend me his. He has a thick skull.'

The only subject he wanted to talk about was Brandon, the only people he wanted to see were the Kinnels. It was Alan's new game. He assumed the air of a spectator helplessly watching a passionate love affair, called Eve 'my poor fellow-sufferer' and smiled meaningly whenever Brandon spoke to Josée. The situation was gradually becoming unbearable, in spite of the combined efforts of Josée and the Kinnels to turn it into a joke. Josée had tried everything: anger, apathy, entreaty. She had even gone off by herself, refusing to see the Kinnels, but Alan found her and spent the afternoon drinking and praising Brandon's charms.

They were supposed to go fishing together that day. Josée had slept badly and looked forward with a kind of savage delight to the moment when Eve, Brandon or she would burst out hysterically. With a little luck, it might happen today.

The Kinnels stood on the jetty with the dejected look they had worn for the past week. Eve held a basket of sandwiches, and with her free hand made what was meant to be a light-hearted gesture. Brandon smiled wanly. The large chriscraft rolled indolently in the small port, the sailor waited.

At that moment Alan stumbled and put his hand to the back of his neck. Brandon came up to him, took his arm:

'What's the matter?'

'The sun,' said Alan. 'I should have brought a hat. I don't feel well.'

He sat on a stone bollard and bent his head. The others looked at one another hesitantly.

'We'll stay here if you don't feel well,' said Josée. 'It would be madness to go out to sea in this sun.'

'No, no, you adore fishing, you three go without me.'

'I'll drive you back home first,' said Brandon. 'You've possibly got a touch of sunstroke and it would be better not to drive.'

'But you would lose an hour's fishing and you're such a keen fisherman. No, much better if Eve drives me home. She hates fishing and would probably prefer to look after me or read aloud to me.'

There was a silence. Brandon turned away and Eve, who was looking at him, thought that she understood.

'That's the best idea. I'm sick of sharks and what not. And after all, you'll be back soon.'

She spoke calmly, and Josée, who was about to protest, said nothing. But she was seething with rage. 'That's just what he wants, the fool. And without running any risks . . . he knows perfectly well that the boat is only a fourteen-footer, and there's a sailor aboard. And there is Eve, looking discreet, and Brandon blushing . . . What does he really want?' She wheeled round and walked up the gang-plank.

'Eve, are you sure . . .' ventured Brandon.

'Why of course, darling. I'll take Alan home. Good fishing to you and don't go too far out, the tide is coming in.'

19

The sailor whistled to himself, impatiently. Brandon reluctantly got into the boat and leaned his elbows on the hand-rail, by Josée. Alan raised his head and looked at them, smiling: he seemed perfectly all right. The boat slowly left the quay.

'Brandon,' said Josée suddenly, 'jump. Jump ashore at once.'

He looked at her, looked at the quay now a yard away, cleared the hand-rail at a leap, slipped and recovered his balance. Eve screamed.

'What's going on?' asked the sailor.

'We're off,' said Josée without turning. She looked Alan straight in the eye. Brandon stood on the quay nervously dusting himself down. Alan no longer smiled. Leaving the hand-rail, she sat in the bow of the boat. The sea was magnificent and she was alone. She had not felt so well for ages.

The basket had of course remained on the quay, so she shared the sailor's food. The fishing had been excellent: two barracudas, each caught after a thirty-minute struggle. And she felt exhausted, famished, delighted. The sailor apparently lived on tomatoes and anchovies, and they joked over the thought of a huge succulent steak. He was very tall, rather loose-limbed, burnt black and had the eyes of a spaniel.

The sky began to cloud over, the sea grew choppy, and on reaching the end of the Keys they decided to turn back. The sailor lowered a line into the sea and Josée took the fishing seat. Sweat streamed unceasingly from their bodies, each staring silently at the sea. Once, she felt a bite, but she struck too late and brought up an empty hook. She called the sailor to ask him for fresh bait.

'My name is Ricardo,' he said.

'And mine, Josée.'

'You're French?'

'Yes.'

'What about the man on the quay?'

He said the man, not 'your husband'. Key Largo was evidently not an island where couples were asked to show their marriage lines. She laughed.

'He's American.'

'He doesn't like fishing?'

'No. Sunstroke.'

Since putting out to sea that morning they had not spoken of their strange departure. He bent his head. His hair was cropped short and very thick. He baited the huge hook very quickly. Then he lit a cigarette and handed it to her. She liked the easy familiarity with which people treated one another in this part of the world.

'Do you like fishing by yourself?'

'I like being by myself now and then.'

'I'm always by myself. I like it better that way.'

He stood behind her. She vaguely thought that he might have been lashing the tiller and that it was not a very wise thing to do with the sea growing rougher.

'You're hot,' he said, and laid his hand on Josée's shoulder.

She turned. He looked at her steadily with pensive dog-like eyes and there was nothing threatening or ambiguous about his expression. She examined the hand on her shoulder, it was large, square, ill-kept. Her heart beat faster. What disturbed her was that quiet, watchful look, without a trace of embarrassment. 'He'll remove his hand if I tell him to and that will be the end of it.' Her mouth felt dry.

'I'm thirsty,' she said faintly.

He took her by the hand. Two steps separated the deck from the cabin. The sheets were clean and Ricardo very brutal. Afterwards, they found a wretched fish hooked on the line and Ricardo laughed like a child.

'Poor thing ... we weren't bothering much about him ...'

His laugh was infectious and she began laughing with him. He held her by the shoulder. She was in a happy mood and did not remind herself that this was the first time she had been unfaithful to Alan.

'Are French fish as stupid?' asked Ricardo.

'No. They're smaller and much more wily.'

'I'd like to go to France and see Paris.'

'And the Eiffel Tower?'

'And the French girls. I'll start the engine again.'

They returned slowly. The sea had calmed down, the sky was tinged a livid pink by a storm that had failed to develop. Ricardo steered, turning now and then to smile at her.

'A thing like this has never happened to me before in all my life,' thought Josée and smiled back at him. Before they landed he asked if she would go fishing again and she said no, that she was leaving soon. He stood on deck for a moment and she looked back at him once.

On the landing-stage, she was told that her husband and Mr and Mrs Kinnel were waiting for her in the bar at Sam's. The Chevrolet had remained where it was. She joined them after taking a shower and changing her dress. In the mirror, she thought she looked ten years younger and had recovered the half-mischievous, half-embarrassed expression that had been hers in Paris from time to time. 'An exasperated woman is easy game,' she said to the glass, quoting an old saying of her closest friend, Bernard P.

They greeted her in polite silence, the two men rising a little too hastily. Eve gave her the ghost of a smile. They had spent the afternoon playing cards and seemed to have had a dull time of it. She talked about her two barracudas, was congratulated, and the conversation died. She made no attempt to revive it. Seated with her head bowed, she was staring at their hands, involuntarily counting their fingers. When she realized what she was doing, she burst out laughing. They jumped.

'What's the matter with you?'

'Nothing. I was just counting your fingers.'

'Well, at any rate, you've come back in good form, whereas Brandon has been dull as ditchwater the whole afternoon.'

'Brandon?' She had forgotten about Alan's game. 'Why?'

'You made him abandon ship. Don't you remember?'

Strangely enough, all three looked annoyed.

'Oh yes, of course. The fact was that I didn't want Eve to spend the day alone with you. You never can tell . . .'

'You're trying to turn the tables,' said Alan.

'There are four of us,' she said gaily, 'enough to make crossed lines. Don't you think so, Eve?'

Eve looked at her in bewilderment and did not reply.

'But since you were eaten up with jealousy, and completely obsessed by the idea of Brandon and me cosily angling for little fishes together, you wouldn't have paid any attention to Eve, and she would have been horribly bored. So I sent Brandon back. That's all. What are we going to eat?'

Brandon nervously stubbed out his cigarette. He did not like her making fun – even imaginary fun – of the wonderful day they might have spent together. For an instant she felt sorry for him, but she was wound up and could not stop.

'Your jokes are in exquisite taste,' said Alan. 'I hope Eve finds them amusing.'

'I still have a good one in reserve,' said Josée, 'I know you'll find it wildly funny. I'm keeping it for dessert.'

She no longer made any attempt to control herself. She had found again the wild euphoria, the taste for violent, irreparable gestures that had been for years a permanent element of her nature. She felt inside her the laughter, the freedom, the glorious detachment of an earlier existence bursting once more into life. She rose from her seat and went to the kitchen.

They dined in heavy silence broken only by Josée's jokes, her holiday reminiscences and her reflections about food. The Kinnels finally thawed and began to laugh too. Alan remained completely silent. He stared at her and drank a great deal.

'Here comes the dessert,' said Josée suddenly, and she felt herself turn pale.

The waiter brought in a round cake topped by a single candle and placed it on the table.

'One candle,' said Josée. 'It's to celebrate the first time I've been unfaithful to you.'

They sat petrified, looking from Josée to the candle, as though trying to solve a riddle.

'The sailor on the boat,' she said impatiently. 'Ricardo.'

Alan got up, hesitated. Josée looked at him, then lowered her eyes. He went out slowly.

'Josée . . .' said Eve. 'What a very bad joke.'

'Not at all. Alan understood it perfectly.'

She picked up a cigarette and her hand shook. It took Brandon a full minute to find his lighter and snap it open.

'What were we talking about?' asked Josée.

She felt exhausted.

*

The door of the car shut with a bang and Josée stood by it, wavering. The Kinnels looked at her silently. Not a light in the house. Yet the Chevrolet was there.

'He must be asleep,' said Eve, without much conviction.

Josée shrugged her shoulders. No, he was not asleep. He was waiting for her. There would be a monumental scene. She had a horror of scenes, of any kind of conflict and, where Alan was concerned, of words. However, she had only herself to blame. 'I'm a fool,' she thought, as she had so often before, 'a complete fool. Why couldn't I keep my mouth shut . . . ?' She turned despairingly to Brandon.

'I don't think I'll be able to stand it,' she said. 'Take me to the airport, Brandon, lend me the money for the fare, I'm going back to France.'

'You can't do that,' said Eve. 'It would be so . . . er . . . cowardly.'

'Cowardly, cowardly . . . What on earth does that mean? I'm only trying to avoid a useless scene, that's all. You're talking like a boy scout. Cowardly . . .'

She spoke under her breath, desperately trying to find some way out. Someone was about to censure her, someone who had every right to do so. That was an idea she had never been able to accept.

'He must be waiting for you,' said Brandon. 'He must be very much shaken by all this.'

All three whispered. They looked like terrified conspirators.

'All right,' said Josée, 'I can't go on dithering. I'd better go in.'

'Would you like us to stick around a little while?'

Brandon had a look of tragic nobility. 'My old beau's forgiven me,' thought Josée, 'but with a bleeding heart.' She smiled swiftly.

'He won't kill me,' she said, and as she saw the Kinnels' horrified expression added emphatically: 'And even if . . .'

She waved good-bye to them and turned away, resignedly. In Paris, things would have happened differently: she would have spent the night with gay easygoing friends and then at dawn she would have gone home too exhausted to be terrified of a scene. But here, she had lingered with two stern critics, and whatever courage she possessed had gradually seeped away. 'Perhaps he *will* kill me,' she thought, 'he's crazy enough.' But she did not really believe it. He would be delighted, would seize avidly on such a good excuse to torment himself. He would insist on knowing every detail, every detail, every . . .'

'My God,' she sighed, 'what on earth am I doing here?'

She wanted her mother, her home, her old surroundings, her friends. She had tried to be sophisticated, to travel, to marry, to leave her country. She had believed it possible to make a fresh start. And now, on a hot night in Florida, leaning against the door of that bamboo house, she felt like sobbing, calling for help, behaving like a child of ten.

She pushed open the door, paused in the darkness. Perhaps he really was asleep. Perhaps she could tiptoe to bed without his hearing her. A wild feeling of hope swept over her. The way it was when she came back from school with a disastrous report, when she stood on the doormat listening to the confused sounds inside the house. Were her parents giving a dinner party? If so, she was saved. The impression was exactly the same and she vaguely realized that she felt no more frightened now of an outraged husband than she had been, fifteen years earlier, of parents who were not particularly bothered by a nought for geography, even though it had been earned by their only daughter. Perhaps there existed a limit for uneasy consciences, for the dread of consequences, and perhaps you reached it once and for all at the stage of twelve. Her hand went up to the electric switch and turned on the light. Alan was sitting on the sofa, looking at her.

'Ah, there you are,' she said stupidly.

And she bit her lip. The retort was easy enough, but he spared her. He looked pale and there was no sign of a bottle anywhere near him.

'What are you doing in the dark?' she went on.

And she sat down meekly a few yards from him. He swept his hand over his eyes, as he often did, and she felt a sudden urge to put her arms around his neck, to comfort him, to say that she had lied. But she did not move.

'I've called up my lawyer,' said Alan in a calm voice. 'I told him I wanted a divorce. He advised me to go to Reno or somewhere. On grounds of mutual misconduct, or just mine, as you like.'

'Oh,' said Josée.

She felt stunned and relieved at the same time, but could not take her eyes off him.

'After what's happened, I think it's the best thing to do,' said Alan.

He rose and put on a record.

She nodded assent. He turned round so quickly that she jumped.

'Don't you agree?'

'I said "yes", at least, I nodded "yes".'

The music filled the room and involuntarily she found herself trying to recognize it. Grieg, Schumann? There were two concertos that she always muddled up.

'I also called up my mother. I let her know – very briefly – how things stood and told her what I'd decided to do. She approved.'

Josée did not reply. She looked at him, and the face she made signified: 'That doesn't surprise me.'

'She even said that she was glad to see me behaving like a man at last,' added Alan almost inaudibly.

His back was turned, she could not see his expression but imagined what it must be like. She made a hesitant move in his direction, then stopped.

'Like a man! . . .' repeated Alan pensively. 'Can you imagine? That's what got me. Honestly –' and he turned to her – 'honestly, do you think it's behaving like a man to leave the only woman you've ever loved just because she spent half an hour in the arms of a shark fisherman?'

He put the question to her candidly, exactly as he would

have put it to an old friend, without a trace of resentment or irony in his voice. 'There's something about him that I like,' thought Josée, 'something crazy that I like.'

'I don't know,' she answered. 'No, I don't think so really.'

'You're being objective, aren't you? I'm sure of that. You're capable of being objective about anything and everything. That's one of the reasons why I love you so much. And so deeply.'

She got up. They stood face to face, looking at each other with a deeper recognition. He placed his arms on her shoulders and she slid between them to lay her cheek against his sweater.

'I want you to stay. Of course I won't forgive you,' he said. 'I'll never forgive you.'

'I know,' she replied.

'There'll be no going back and starting again from the beginning, bygones won't be bygones. I'm not what my mother understands by a man, and you know it?'

'Yes, I know,' she said, and felt like crying.

'You're tired, so am I. What's more, I've lost my voice. I had to shout to make myself heard in New York. Can you imagine me yelling: "My wife has been unfaithful to me. No, no, unfaithful. U for . . ." Ludicrous, isn't it?'

'Yes,' she said, 'ludicrous. Now all I want is to go to sleep.'

He released her, took off the record and put it away carefully before turning to her:

'Was he good in bed? Do tell me . . . how was he?'

*

It was nearly the end of September. They should have been back in New York, but neither of them alluded to it. Alan loathed 'other people', and Josée certainly preferred being alone with him to putting up with the outbursts of jealousy which were aroused by the slightest look or the slightest remark if it was not directly addressed to him. In this respect his plan had worked. America, Europe melted away into a haze, and nothing remained of her life but Alan's anxious face, a face increasingly hollow and tanned. The Kinnels lingered on, too, but the tempo of conversation had slackened. Alan showed an odd contempt for Brandon since the business of Ricardo: 'If that ass hadn't jumped down like a lap-dog when you told him to . . .' and Josée did not even attempt to point out the absurdity of his argument. Besides, she was tired of talking about Ricardo, of answering Alan's innumerable questions about Ricardo's character and of snapping 'no!' when he asked her if she were thinking about Ricardo. She had given up thinking altogether, she was sick of the sun, she bitterly regretted that Alan was not obliged to go to an office from nine to five; she missed the thick sweaters of the north, and spent her time in the semi-darkness of her air-conditioned room reading detective stories. Apart from this, she was calm, smiling, apathetic. She thought that she would die in Florida, some fine day, without anyone, including herself, knowing why. Alan hovered round her, asking questions about her past life, about Paris, which invariably ended, via Ricardo, bad language and insults, in love on the bamboo bed. It was all as she knew it would be. She watched it all happening as the bird watches the proverbial snake – only in her case the bird was disenchanted, if birds can be.

'You must like it, deep down in your heart of hearts,' he said to her once. The idea appalled her. Perhaps in the end she had really come to like it, to enjoy being treated as the unresisting object of a morbid love and not as an independent human being. She wondered about it all night, recognized that she was hypnotized and no longer had the strength to fight back. But she didn't like it. No.

She did not like a man to be obsessed by her: what she wanted was to share his life. And she certainly felt no longer the inane pride such an obsession had once aroused.

One evening, she plucked up courage enough to beg Alan to let her go away by herself for a couple of weeks, no matter where. He refused.

'I can't live without you. If you want to leave me, leave me. Give me up completely or not at all.'

'I'll leave you.'

'Of course you will, some day. Meanwhile, I'm not going to inflict two weeks of torture on myself for nothing. I've got you, and I intend to make the most of it.'

He laughed. She could not bring herself to hate him. She dared not leave him. She was frightened. She had never done anything important enough in life to justify in her own eyes the luxury of being responsible for someone's death or downfall. Or even despair. No doubt she was 'ruining' her life, as Brandon said, but had she ever done anything else, so far? 'But I've been very happy,' she said to herself, but of what value was that? A relatively decent life, loyal friends, a happy temperament; scarcely enough to stand up to the obsession of a man of thirty.

'It's not as if we're happy.'

'We are at times, a little,' he said, and it was true. 'In any case, we'll see it through. I'll wear you down, I'll wear myself down, I'll never let up, not for a moment. Two human beings ought to be able to live tightly, breathlessly clutched to one another. That's called love.'

'Two human beings stinking with money,' she said. 'If you had to work . . .'

'The question doesn't arise, thank God. And if I had to work, I'd be a fisherman and take you along with me on my boat. You have a soft spot for fishermen, it seems . . .'

And everything would begin again. Everything began again, but it was never like anything she had known before.

Alan had one quality more impressive than all his defects: he was detached. Self-detached to the point of trying to commit suicide one winter – only a slight mishap had prevented him. And then he was not in the least in love with himself, never cherished himself in the revolting way that other people do. He did not even think much of himself. He had no defence against her. His attitude simply was: 'I want you and if you leave me, nothing can comfort me, not even the pleasure of crying.' He scared her. For he was indifferent to his own good looks, while she enjoyed being attractive, indifferent to money, while she enjoyed spending, indifferent to existing, while she enjoyed life. His indifference broke down before her alone. And in such a famished . . . such a morbid way.

'You should have been a queer,' she said. 'With your mother as a cause, your looks and your money as means, you would have been the rage of Capri.'

'And you would have had a quiet life . . . but the thing is that I've always liked women. Or rather . . . I've always had women. Until you. Before you, I never really loved anything. So you have really been the first body to really mean anything.'

She looked at him, a little bewildered. She had certainly loved other men besides Alan, other bodies particularly. Nights in Paris and on the beaches of the Mediterranean had left their mark on her: delicate marks of use which he hated, but which she refused to disavow. What she considered indecent in Alan's attitude was that he laid bare his own chilly, comfortable past and took a certain pride in it. No, he did not really feel pride in it. In fact, he had no sense of direction, no idea of what to make of his life. He drifted from crisis to crisis, sensation to sensation, like an invalid or a completely honest person. And she could not make out which of the two he was; nor how, in the first alternative, she had a right to say: 'Look here, you're a human being, you must try to get well.' Nor could she, in the second alternative, convince him that he was going about it the wrong way, that small concessions had to be made to society, pious frauds committed – and although such frauds were certainly necessary, she was not sure that they were justified. People who talked about the Absolute disgusted her even more than those who never gave it a thought. Alan never talked about it.

Their best moments were always in the middle of the night, after they had flayed one another, according to a well-established pattern, when exhaustion softened Alan's face, turned him once again into the stammering little boy which he should never have ceased to be. It was then that she tried to talk to him very gently, to make her words sink into his slumber, into an existence where he was ultimately obliged to live without her for a few hours. She would tell him how strong and sensitive and attractive and exceptional he was, she talked to him about himself, she tried to reconcile him to himself, to make him take an interest in himself. 'Think so?' he would ask in a delighted, childlike voice, and fall asleep close to her. Some morning, she thought, he would wake up in love with himself, independent, and a tiny detail would prove this to her: he would yawn and look for his cigarettes without glancing at her first. Sometimes she pretended to be asleep in order to watch what he did as soon as he stirred. He stretched out his hand convulsively, to make certain she was there, and then, reassured, opened his eyes, raised himself on one elbow to watch her sleeping. One morning when she had got up early to see the dawn, he gave a scream of genuine anguish that made her rush to him. They stared at each other without a word and she got back into bed.

'You're not a man,' she said.

' "To be a man . . ." what does that mean? If it means being brave, I'm brave. Virile too. And selfish.'

'A man should be able to live without constantly needing someone with him, his mother or his wife.'

'I've never needed my mother, and I'm in love with you. You only have to read Proust. And if you need the protection of a man, I'm here too.'

'What I need at present is air, not protection.'

'The air of the open sea? Ricardo?'

She left the room. She went out and stood in the doorway, limp with heat. At times, she cried from weariness and, like a school child, lapped up her tears with her tongue as they ran down her cheek. Then she went in again. Alan would put on a record they both liked, talk about music, which he knew a lot about, and in the end she would answer him. Time passed.

One September day, at the end of the month, they received a telegram. Alan's mother was due to have an operation. They packed, and with heavy hearts they left the house where they had known such happiness.

Pause

3

The white room was strewn with little cellophane boxes in which pallid orchids were beginning to fade. Helen Ash gave her daughter-in-law that famous hawk-like stare of hers – she could not remember which journalist had so described it, but for the last ten years she opened her eyes wide and contracted her nostrils on serious occasions. Josée sighed as she recognized the symptom.

'Well, what's your news? I saw Alan this morning. He looks pretty well, but he's a bundle of nerves.'

'He always has been, I imagine. However, we're all right, Mother. What about you? It seems the operation won't amount to much, will it?'

The hawk-like stare was replaced by an expression of resignation.

'Other people's operations never seem very serious. Even to the next of kin.'

'Nor to the surgeons in this case,' said Josée calmly, 'and that makes me easy in my mind.'

There was a pause. Helen Ash did not like anyone to ruin her act. And that day the act consisted in bequeathing her delicate son to her daughter-in-law before leaving for a fatal operation. She laid her hand on Josée's arm and Josée found herself admiring the rings on it.

'What a glorious sapphire,' she said.

'They'll be yours soon. Indeed they will,' she continued as Josée made a gesture, 'yes indeed, and very soon. They will help you to get over the death of a tiresome old woman.'

She expected Josée to remonstrate, to say something agreeable about her age, health, character, and the affection she inspired in others, but what she got was quite different.

'Oh no,' said Josée getting up, 'please don't you start too. I'm not going to weep and wail over you as well. I suppose there isn't an old uncle in the family who needs some sympathy too?'

'Why, my dear . . . your nerves are on edge, like the rest of us.'

'Yes,' said Josée, 'my nerves are on edge too.'

'Florida . . .'

'Florida has a sunny climate, that's about all.'

'Really all?'

Her intonation surprised Josée. She stared at Helen, who looked down.

'Alan rang me up. Now you can tell me everything, child – just between the two of us.'

'You mean, about Ricardo?'

'Was that his name? Alan was half crazy and . . . Josée . . .'

She had already left and only calmed down again outside. The streets of New York were sunny and noisy, the air was sharp and exciting as ever. 'Ricardo,' she murmured smiling, 'Ricardo . . . that name will drive me mad.' She tried to recall his face and failed. Alan was signing papers for his mother, the only work he would stoop to, of course, and she decided to walk up the avenue.

She recognized the particular smell of New York, the hurry and bustle of the crowd, the sensation of walking again on high heels and she was wearing a beatific smile when she ran into Bernard. They stared at each other with the same amazement before falling into one another's arms.

'Josée . . . I thought you were dead.'

'No, only married.'

He laughed. He had been very much in love with her in Paris a few years before and she remembered him as he was then; lean and dejected, in his old raincoat, saying good-bye to her with tears in his eyes. And there he stood, broader, darker, smiling. Suddenly she felt as though she had recovered her entire family all at once, her whole past, to say nothing of finding her own self again. She began to laugh.

'Bernard, Bernard . . . how wonderful to see you! What are you doing in New York?'

'My book has come out here. You know, I've been awarded a prize – at last.'

'And now you take yourself rather seriously?'

'Very seriously, and I'm in the money too and a womanizer. You know, the man of letters, who has just produced a masterpiece.'

'A masterpiece?'

'No, just a best seller, but I never admit it and seldom give it a thought. Let's go and have a drink.'

He took her to a bar. She looked at him and smiled as he talked about Paris, their friends, his success, and once more she recognized the mixture of gaiety and bitterness she had always liked so much in him. She had always thought of him as a sort of brother. This was not what he wanted and once very briefly she had tried to fall in with his desires but that was long, long ago. Meanwhile, there had been Alan. She frowned, and he paused.

'What about you? Your husband? He's American?'

'Yes.'

'Nice, honest, quiet, adoring?'

'I used to think so.'

'Vicious, unbalanced, unscrupulous, cruel, brutal?'

'He's not that either.'

Bernard began laughing.

'Now listen, Josée, I've painted two typical portraits for you. I'm not surprised that you should have found something special, but do explain.'

'Well,' she said, 'he . . .'

And suddenly she burst out sobbing.

She cried for a long time on Bernard's shoulder, a distressed, embarrassed Bernard. She cried for a long time over Alan and herself and over what they had meant to each other and over what had ended or was about to end. For this meeting had made her realize what she had refused to face for the last six months: that she had made a mistake. And she set herself too high a standard, she was too proud to be able to fool herself any longer. The far too tender nightmare was over.

Meanwhile, Bernard wiped her face with his handkerchief, muttering indistinct remarks and threats concerning the dirty lowdown bum, etc. . . .

'I'm going to leave him,' she said at last.

'Do you love him?'

'No.'

'Then stop crying. Don't talk, have a drink or you'll be completely dehydrated. You're much prettier, you know.'

She began laughing, then took his hand in hers.

'When do you go back?'

'In ten days. Are you going back with me?'

'Yes. Don't let me out of your sight for the next ten days, or at least, as little as possible.'

'I've got to fit in a broadcast, between two advertisements for shoes, but that's my only engagement. I meant to take it easy. You must show me New York.'

'Fine. Come and have a drink this evening. You'll see Alan and you can tell him that this can't go on any longer. Perhaps he'll listen to you and . . .'

Bernard jumped.

'You're as crazy as ever. It's your job to talk to him.'

'I can't.'

'Now listen, divorce isn't a very serious business in America.'

Then she tried to talk to him about Alan, but Bernard, with his logical French mind, talked about common sense, psychopathology and an immediate divorce.

'I'm all he has,' she said despairingly.

'That's a silly remark,' began Bernard, then stopped, and after a moment continued:

'Sorry, there must still be some remnants of jealousy left in me. I'll see you this evening. And don't worry, I'm with you.'

His last remark would have made her smile two years earlier, but now it reassured her. There was no doubt that success, whether he believed in it or not, had steadied Bernard. And also, she had asked him to protect her and he had found her as attractive as ever. They parted, mutually impressed.

*

Alan stood before the mirror putting on his tie, surprisingly handsome in his dark suit. She was ready first and was waiting for him. It was one of Alan's manias to watch her dress and make up, to get in her way, to hinder her under the guise of helping her, then narcissistically to change his own clothes while she watched him. Once again she admired the bronze torso, narrow hips, sturdy neck, thinking that very soon they would no longer belong to her and wondering with a sort of shame if she would not miss all this beauty as much as the rest.

'Where shall we dine?'

'Wherever you like.'

'Oh, I forgot to tell you that I met one of my old friends from France, Bernard Palig. He writes novels and his latest book is coming out here. I asked him to dinner.'

There was a short silence. She wondered why Alan's reactions should seem important to her since she was going to leave him in ten days. But looking at him the fact seemed as impossible as it had seemed inevitable a couple of hours earlier.

'Why didn't you tell me before?'

'I'd forgotten all about it.'

'Isn't he one of your old loves?'

'No.'

'There's never been anything between you? What's the matter with him? Is he one-eyed or something?'

She held her breath for a second. She could feel a noose of anger tightening and gathering inside her, and she counted the pulsations of the artery in her throat, which had suddenly started to pound. She just prevented herself saying: 'I'm getting a divorce,' in a flat, decisive tone of voice. Then she remembered that you don't walk out on someone through spite and that she was going to hurt Alan quite enough as it was.

'He's not one-eyed,' she replied, 'he's very sweet and I know you'll like him.'

Alan stood motionless, holding his clumsily knotted tie between his fingers. He raised his eyes to hers in the mirror, astonished by the gentleness in her voice.

'Forgive me,' he said. 'It's already sad enough that jealousy should make me stupid, but it's quite inexcusable that it should make me so rude.'

'Don't become human,' thought Josée, 'don't start to change, don't disarm me or take away my reasons for leaving you. Don't do that to me.' Then perhaps she would no longer have the courage to leave him, and leave him she must. She positively must. Now that her mind was made up, that she had had a taste of life without him, she lived in a state of complete dizziness that wanted to spill over into words. So long as those words had not been spoken, nothing was settled, her decision did not really exist.

'In fact, I did have an affair with him. It lasted three days.'

'Ah!' said Alan, 'he's the writer from the provinces. I forget his name.'

'Bernard Palig.'

'You told me about it one evening. You went to see him to tell him his wife needed him and stayed on at the hotel. Isn't that the one?'

'Yes,' she answered, 'that's the one.'

She suddenly had a picture of the greyish square at Poitiers, the shabby paper on the walls of the room and, again, breathed in the smell of the provinces. She smiled. All that was to be hers again: the gentle hills of the Île-de-France, the neat little gardens, the old houses, the air of Paris streets, the golden Mediterranean, all the images that crowded her memory.

'I didn't remember that I'd told you.'

'You've told me lots and lots of things. The only things I don't know about you are what you have forgotten yourself. I've dragged everything out of you.'

He turned towards her. It seemed years since she had seen him dressed in a suit, and this man in dark blue, these hard eyes in a child's face, were suddenly alien to her. 'Alan,' a voice said inside her, but she did not move.

'It's impossible to drag anything out of anyone,' she said. 'Don't worry. And please don't be boorish with Bernard. You can be so sweet when you try.'

'Your friends are my friends.'

They did not take their eyes off one another. She began laughing.

'Hostile . . . That's what we've become. Hostile to one another.'

'Yes, but *I* love you,' said Alan in a polite voice. 'We'll go and wait for your friend in the library.'

He took her arm and involuntarily she leaned on him. How long had she been leaning on that arm? A year, two years? She no longer remembered and suddenly felt frightened that her arm might miss his, that she might never know again where to lay her hand. Security . . . ironically enough, this neurotic man was her security.

Bernard arrived punctually and they had cocktails and talked politely about New York. Josée had fancied she was about to witness the impact of two worlds, of her two worlds, but, as it turned out, she was simply drinking a Martini with two men of about the same build, equally well-mannered, who had once had, or who still had, a strong feeling for her. Alan smiled, and Bernard's expression, which had been rather condescending when he arrived, quickly changed to one of annoyance. She tended to forget how unusually good-looking Alan was and felt an odd pride in the fact. So much so that she neglected to keep her eye on the cocktail shaker, and it was only when she caught an expressive signal from Bernard that she turned round to see what Alan was up to. He was fumbling with a packet of cigarettes in an attempt to get one out.

'Shall we go and have dinner?' she said.

'One last drink,' suggested Alan pleasantly, and he turned to Bernard who refused.

'But I insist,' Alan continued. 'But I insist.' The atmosphere had suddenly become tense. 'I really insist.' Bernard got up.

'No, thanks, I'd much rather go and eat.'

'Not until you've drunk a toast with me,' said Alan. 'You can't refuse.'

'If Bernard doesn't want to,' began Josée, but Alan interrupted her.

'Well, Bernard?'

They stood and faced each other. 'Alan is more athletic, but he's drunk,' thought Josée swiftly. 'And anyway, I can't remember if Bernard is tough or not. But it's scarcely the moment for a study in comparative anatomy.' She took the glass from Alan's hand.

'I'll drink with you. And so will Bernard. What to?'

'To Poitiers,' said Alan, and drained his glass at a gulp. Bernard raised his glass.

'To Key Largo,' he said. 'One kind thought deserves another.'

'To this charming gathering,' said Josée, and burst out laughing.

All three returned at dawn from Harlem. The sky-scrapers stood out sharply against the mist rising from Central Park, and in the cold air the yellow leaves seemed to have found a fresh vigour.

'What a beautiful city!' said Bernard under his breath. Josée nodded. She sat sandwiched with one on each side, as she had the entire evening.

They settled her between them, danced with her one after the other, like automatons. For once, Alan drank in moderation and made no further allusions to awkward subjects. Bernard seemed a little less tense, but she could not recall having spoken directly to him – or he to her. 'It's a dog's life,' she thought, 'a real dog's life. And a life that people might possibly envy me.' Alan let down a window to throw away a cigarette, and cold air swept into the taxi.

'It's cold,' he said. 'It's cold everywhere.'

'Except in Florida,' she said.

'Even in Florida.' He turned so suddenly towards him that Bernard started. 'My dear Bernard,' he said, 'let's forget the young woman sitting between us for a second. I'll forget you're a logical Frenchman and you'll forget I belong to the privileged class.'

Bernard shrugged his shoulders. 'How strange,' thought

Josée, 'he knows I'm leaving Alan and going back to Paris when he does and he's the one who looks annoyed.'

'There,' said Alan, 'everything has been forgotten and now we can talk a little. Driver!' he cried, 'find a bar, anywhere you can.'

'I'm sleepy,' said Josée.

'You can be sleepy later. Now, I've got to talk to my friend Bernard who has the Latin idea of love and can throw some light on our relationship. Also, I'm thirsty.'

They found themselves in a small, deserted bar on Broadway, the *Boccage*, and the name with its spelling mistake made Josée smile. And what idea could the proprietor possibly have of the wooded downlands of Normandy called *bocage*? Was it merely the sound of these two syllables which had caught his fancy? Alan ordered three glasses of brandy and threatened to drink all three if they took anything else.

'So now we've forgotten Josée,' he said. 'I don't know you, I'm just a drunk you've picked up in a bar who's been boring you stiff with his life story. Suppose I call you Jean, that's a typical French name.'

'All right, call me Jean,' said Bernard.

He was ready to drop with sleep.

'What are your views on love, my dear Jean?'

'I have none,' said Bernard, 'absolutely none.'

'That's not true, Jean. I've read your work or at least one volume of it. You have a wealth of ideas about love. Well, I'm in love. With a woman. With my wife. I love her with a sadistic, devouring passion. What must I do? She is thinking of leaving me.'

Josée looked at him, looked at Bernard who was waking up.

'If she's leaving you and you know why, I can't see what there is for me to say.'

'Let me explain what I believe. Love is something that

has to be sought for. People look for it in pairs, and it usually happens that only one of the pair gets hold of it. In this case, it was me. My wife was delighted. She came up to me like a doe to eat this tender, inexhaustible fruit out of my hand. She was the only doe that I could bear to feed.'

He swallowed his drink at a gulp, smiled at Josée.

'You must excuse such comparisons, my dear Jean. Americans are apt to become poetical. Anyway, my wife gorged herself, my wife now wants something else or won't stand being forcibly fed. And yet, I still have that fruit, it weighs heavy in my hand and I want to give it to her. What am I to do?'

'You might imagine that she also has a fruit in her hand and that . . . those comparisons of yours get on my nerves, anyway. Instead of always insisting on being the one to give, you might have thought that she had something to give too, you might have tried to understand her, how should I know . . .'

'You're married, aren't you, my dear Jean?'

'Yes,' said Bernard, and stiffened.

'And your wife loves you and feeds you. And you do not leave her, although she bores you.'

'You seem very well informed.'

'And you do not leave her because of what you call pity, isn't that it?'

'That's none of your business,' said Bernard. 'It's you we're talking about.'

'I'm talking about love,' said Alan. 'That calls for a celebration. Barman . . .'

'Stop drinking,' said Josée in a low voice.

She felt ill. It was true that she had fed on Alan's love, had found in it a reason for living – or a means of passing the time, she thought furtively. It was also true that she was worn out, that she no longer wanted to be 'forcibly fed' as he expressed it. Alan continued:

45

'And so you are bored with your wife, my dear Jean. Long ago you loved Josée, or at least you thought you did, and she gave in to you and you two played a sentimental and melancholy duet in the same key. For your violins are perfectly attuned, that is, in a minor key.'

'If you like,' said Bernard.

He looked at Josée, and neither of them smiled. At that moment, she would have given anything to have loved him passionately, in order to have some defence against Alan's remarks. Bernard seemed to understand and blushed.

'What about you, Alan? What have *you* done? You've loved a woman and poisoned her life.'

'Well, that's something, anyway. Do you suppose somebody else could fill it?'

They turned to her. She got up slowly.

'This discussion fascinates me. Go on with it, since you've forgotten all about me. I'm going to bed.'

She was outside the bar before they could rise to their feet, and found a taxi at once. She gave the driver the address of a hotel she had once heard of.

'It's late,' murmured the driver with the air of a connoisseur, 'it's too late to go to bed.'

'Yes,' she agreed, 'it's much too late.'

And suddenly, she saw herself running away in a taxi, at twenty-seven, leaving a husband who loved her, crossing New York at dawn and saying very gravely: 'It's too late.' She told herself that as long as she lived, she would never be able to resist rehearsing situations, staging them, 'seeing herself' from the outside. She told herself that she should have been weeping in the taxi or becoming panic-stricken instead of vaguely wondering if the driver's name – nailed to the seat according to regulations – were really Silvius Marcus.

It was only after ordering a plane ticket for Paris, a toothbrush and some toothpaste, all to be delivered that afternoon – it was only when she lay curled up in bed, daylight vaguely stealing into the anonymous room, that she began shivering with cold, fatigue, and loneliness. She was used to sleeping by Alan, and during the half-hour it took her to fall asleep she saw her own life as a huge disaster.

4

A terrific wind snapped the branches of trees, lifting them for a moment, free and transfigured, before dropping them, rolling them in the grass and finally embedding them in the mud where they stuck for good. Standing at the door, Josée looked at the lawn, the yellowish fields and the chestnut trees threshing and plying. A large branch suddenly broke off from the trunk with a tearing sound, and seemed to leap in the air, leaves folded back by the wind, and fell at Josée's feet. 'Icarus,' she said, and picked it up. It was cold. She entered the house and went up to her room. The floor was tiled and there was no furniture except for a table littered with newspapers and a huge wardrobe. She laid the branch on her bed, the stump on the pillow and admired it for a second; bruised, torn, yellowing. It looked like a dead seagull or a funeral wreath – the very image of desolation.

For the past two weeks she had idled in the Norman countryside laid waste by a savage autumn. On reaching Paris, she had immediately rented the lonely old house from a delighted estate agent, much as she might have rented a place in Touraine or in any other province. No one had been told of her arrival: she wished to regain possession of herself. There was a certain irony in the term, for there was nothing to regain, much less herself. She had come across the idea too often in too many novels. Here, there was the wind that snatched up and dropped everything, the delights of a wood fire in the evening, of all the earth's scents and smells and of solitude. Life in the country. But she must still be very young or very romantic to have imagined so fondly, in the aeroplane which brought her back to France, this house in the country where she could reconstruct her life, piece herself together again. Nothing had been demolished, nothing lost, not even time, and she was forced to recognize her own toughness of mind and body in spite of all the regrets, all the heartbreaking memories. She could stay here for as long as she liked, provided that she was prepared to put up with boredom. Or return to Paris and begin again. Begin once more to look for the fruit that Alan spoke of, or for a certain standard of material comfort, or for a job, or for a good time. She could also go walking in the wind, or put on a record, or read. She was free. It was neither unpleasant nor exciting, it was merely that unquenchable optimism of hers, the only constant element of her nature.

She could not remember ever having felt desperate, but merely depressed, at times to the point of dull stupefaction. She remembered sobbing over a dead cat, her old Siamese who had died of typhus, it must have been four years before. She remembered the violence of her grief, the sort of horrible inward rasping that resolved itself in tears. She remembered having deliberately dwelt on the cat's playful ways, its naps in front of the fire, its trustingness. Yes, that was the worst thing of all: the disappearance of a creature that completely trusted you, that put its life in your hands. It must be unbearable to lose a child, perhaps even more so to lose a jealous husband. Alan . . . what was Alan doing? Wandering about New York, from bar to bar? Or did he go to his psychiatrist every day, hand in hand with his mother? Or, simpler still, was he sleeping with a compassionate little American girl? None of that satisfied her. She would have liked to know.

She spoke to no one but the gardener's wife, a woman from Picardy who did the housework and slept in, for

Josée was afraid of the dark. From time to time, she went to the village for no particular reason, just to talk French and buy newspapers that she skimmed through without reading. Her arrival in Paris, after two years of absence, had been incredible. She had spent three days wandering about the streets, sleeping in various hotels, dazed to find that nothing had changed. Her old apartment still seemed empty. People looked exactly the same. She had met no one, rung no one up, and then a yearning for the country came over her so swiftly that she hired a car and ran away. Her parents must think that she was still in Florida. Perhaps Bernard and Alan were searching New York for her while she read Conan Doyle, solitary in her house. It was all absurd. But only the wind seemed really serious in its fury, it alone seemed to have a definite aim, a precise destination. Later, when it calmed down, the gardener would pick up its victims from the lawn and burn them. The sweet smell of burning leaves would seep in through the window, tear her away from the adventures of Sherlock Holmes, subject her once more to their nostalgic influence, like the smell of the earth at night, like the touch of rough sheets smelling of moth-balls, like everything that recalled her youth – a youth so near and already so remote and, as it were, embalmed. A dog scratched at the door: the farm dog had taken a fancy to her and spent hours with his head on her knees. He drooled a little, unfortunately. She let him in and, through a window in the passage, saw the postman. This was the first time he had called.

The telegram said: 'Await you urgently Paris. Fondest love. Bernard.' She sat on the bed, and as she absent-mindedly stroked the dead branch she thought she would have a coat made of the same colour. The dog looked at her.

Paris

5

'I know how your mind works, my dear. You wanted to be alone and you longed for the provinces. So you had to rent something. As you always do everything in the simplest way, you opened the classified directory of estate agents and rang the first one printed in black type. You asked about houses in the country that you could take by the month. To find where you were, I did the same thing. Only you rang the second estate agent. How did that happen?'

'The first number was engaged,' said Josée gloomily.

Bernard gave a shrug, rather pleased with himself.

'That occurred to me. When I was told that a crazy girl had taken an unheated house in Normandy for October, I knew it was you. I even thought of coming to fetch you.'

'And then?'

'And then, I didn't dare. Your departure had been rather brutal. Alan and I spent the next day scouring New York. By the afternoon we were in a pretty state. He thought of Air France, but an hour too late.'

'So what did you do then?'

'We took the next one. The next plane. I skipped my radio talk and was barely able to get my luggage.'

'Is Alan here?'

She had risen. Bernard made her sit down again.

'Don't bolt. He's been here for the past two weeks. At the Ritz, needless to say. He's put Sherlock Homes and Lemmy Caution on your track . . .'

'Sherlock Holmes,' she repeated, 'that's funny, I've just been reading . . .'

'I may be less ingenious than Sherlock Holmes, but I know your habits. So for God's sake you've got to do something. Get a divorce or run away to Brazil. But don't leave me with Alan on my hands. He's with me every minute. He feels almost friendly to me, but he'll start hating me again if he sees you looking at me. I'm exhausted.'

He threw himself back on the divan. They were in a small Left Bank hotel where Josée had once lived for a while. She shook him roughly.

'You're not going to complain, are you? Two weeks...! Why, I've been with him for eighteen months.'

'Yes, but for you there were compensations that I can't really be expected to share.'

She hesitated and burst out laughing. Her laughter was infectious, and for a few minutes they were doubled up on the divan, moaning and hiccoughing with mirth, their eyes full of tears.

'You're fantastic,' said Bernard, choking. 'Quite fantastic. You're going to blame me for your marriage, me, who was madly in love with you ... and probably still am ... And who has been holding your husband's hand for the last two weeks ... it's incredible ...'

'Do shut up,' said Josée. 'I must stop laughing. I must think things over. That's what I wanted to do in the country ... If only you could have seen me ... I thought about nothing, I just shivered ... and also a ravishing dog lived there ... he used to slobber over me ...'

They went off into fresh bouts of laughter at the thought of the dog and ended by facing each other, exhausted and crimson. Bernard had a handkerchief which they shared like children.

'What am I going to do?' asked Josée.

Alan was now in the same place as she, quite close, and her beating heart turned into something precious, burdensome, impossible to restrain.

'If you want a divorce, go and see a lawyer. That's all. He can't kill you.'

'I'm not thinking of myself, but of him . . . I don't know.'

'Well, I do, now,' said Bernard. 'He's a funny guy. When I'm not with him and I think of him wandering round Paris alone, it makes me turn quite cold. He seems to have aroused maternal instincts in me that I didn't know I had until I met him.'

'He affects you like that too?'

'But that doesn't seem to me a sufficient basis for marriage,' said Bernard severely. 'But that's your affair. Meanwhile why don't you come to Séverin's cocktail party this evening? He won't be there. I must be off. Alan's at the Ritz if you want to reach him. With fifteen elderly English spinsters simply eating him up.'

Worried and hesitant, Josée leaned against the door, then tackled her luggage. Unpacking would fill a couple of hours at least, prevent her from thinking until it was time for the cocktail party. And there she was sure to find someone to advise her, someone full of principles and definite ideas. 'I really am unbelievably weak,' she thought. 'I'm the one who should determine my life.' But her life was like a confused, futile scuffle – she thought of Bernard's uncontrollable laughter and smiled at herself in the mirror. Then she remembered the short sentence he had lightly dropped: 'I was madly in love with you and probably still am . . .' She picked up a hanger and carefully slipped a dress on it. A pretty dress and most becoming. Yes, people loved her, but she contributed nothing to the love she aroused. She just nibbled out of other people's hands. She disliked herself.

*

Séverin's cocktail parties were the most successful of their

53

kind. As usual there were some very rich people, some very entertaining ones, an exotic actor or two, several personalities from artistic and literary circles, a decent proportion of homosexuals, all old friends. Josée was delighted to find herself back in the corrupt, artificial, hollow little world that was also the liveliest, freest, gayest little world of any capital city on earth.

She knew a number of people who, after two years of absence, greeted her with shrieks of joy that were only half exaggerated, as if they had seen her the day before. Throwing their arms round her neck they kissed her, following the French custom that dated, according to Séverin, from the liberation.

Séverin was fifty, had read too much Huxley and took himself for a satyr let loose in society. His flat was littered with photographs of magnificent women that no one knew and about whom he proved unusually discreet. He always laughed a little too loudly to emphasize his vitality and was bemused by dawn, but genuine kindness and generosity, as well as an unceasing flow of whisky, made him plenty of real friends. Josée was one of them. After he had kissed her six times and proposed marriage, according to a well-established ritual, he drew her aside, sat her under a lamp and gazed at her intently.

'Let me look at you.'

Josée threw back her head submissively. One of Séverin's most tiresome claims was that he could read everything in a face.

'You've been through a lot of trouble.'

'No, no, Séverin, everything is all right.'

'Secretive as ever. You vanish for a couple of years and then come back, looking charming, without a word of explanation. Where's your husband?'

'At the Ritz,' said Josée, and began laughing.

'So he's the Ritz type?' asked Séverin frowning.

'There must be ten people here this evening who live at the Ritz.'

'That's not the same thing. They aren't married to my closest friend.'

Josée raised her head, the light hurt her eyes.

'Your closest friend is thirsty, Séverin.'

'I'll be right back. Don't budge. You're not to mix with these appalling people. You've just spent two years in America, you're like a savage. They don't know how to talk to savages.'

He gave his great laugh and disappeared. Josée's eyes wandered fondly over these appalling people. They discussed things passionately, burst out laughing, turned from one to another as swiftly as they changed their topic of conversation. They spoke French. She really felt like a savage: two years on an out-of-the-way island with Alan and listening to the Kinnels' ponderous reflections, two years without seeing any other face. Paris was really very pleasant.

'See that woman over there?' asked Séverin, returning to his seat by her. 'Do you recognize her?'

'Wait a minute . . . No, I don't, who is it?'

'Elizabeth. Don't you remember? She used to work on a newspaper, I was crazy about her.'

'My God! But how old can she be?'

'Thirty. Looks fifty, doesn't she? It's one of the most impressive collapses I've seen since you left. In two years. She's head over heels in love with a half-crazy painter of sorts, she's thrown everything over for him, she's given up her job; and she's taken to the bottle. And now to crown it all, he won't have anything to do with her.'

Elizabeth, as though someone had nudged her, turned and gave Séverin a little smile. Her face was at once thin and puffy, and she had the expression of a sick animal.

'Having a good time?' called Séverin.

'I always do at your parties.'

'So that's passion,' thought Josée, 'that's the face of passion, puffy and gaunt, with two rows of pearls under it. God, how I love people . . .' She felt on the crest of the wave. She would have liked to talk for hours to that woman grown suddenly old, to make her talk about herself, to know and understand everything about her. She would have liked to know everything about each person in the room; how they went to sleep, what they dreamed of, what gave them pleasure or caused them fear or pain. For a moment she loved them all, with their ambitions, their vanity, their childish attempts to bolster themselves up, the pathetic sense of loneliness that flickered in each one of them.

'She's going to die,' said Josée.

'She's tried to again and again. Never hard enough. After each attempt he sobs and comes back to her for three days. So why would you expect her really to kill herself? Wait a minute, my orchestra is getting ready. No one can play the Charleston the way they can.'

The Charleston was back in Paris, as in 1925 – but without the gaiety of the twenties, some people complained, while thoroughly enjoying themselves. The pianist settled down, the musicians began to play *Swanee*, and conversation dropped a little. Séverin's inopportune taste for side-shows at unlikely moments was as well known as his Scotch. A thin young man sat down by Josée, introduced himself and immediately added:

'I hope you won't mind if I don't talk to you. I can't bear conversation.'

'That's absurd,' said Josée gaily. 'You shouldn't go to cocktail parties if you don't like talking. And if you're just being original, that won't work here. You've got to be vital at Séverin's parties.'

'I couldn't care less about being original,' answered the young man fiercely, and began to sulk.

Josée felt like laughing. Smoke filled the room, people had to shout to be heard above the conscientious orchestra, the noise was deafening and empty glasses strewed the tables. She longed for Bernard to appear and give her further news of Alan.

'For God's sake,' shouted Séverin, 'please stop chattering for a minute. Robin Douglas has promised to sing two wonderful songs.'

Everyone sat down a trifle sourly, and Séverin turned out most of the lights. A form stumbled and then sat down by Josée. The singer announced mournfully: '*Ole Man River*', someone cried 'bravo', and he began singing. As he was coloured, people were immediately convinced that he had talent, and a dead silence ensued. He sang slowly, bleating a little, and the sullen young man murmured something about the nostalgia of the black soul. Josée, who had roamed Harlem with Alan, felt less enthusiastic, and yawned. Leaning back, she glanced at her right-hand neighbour. First she saw a highly polished black shoe gleaming in the half-light, then a trouser crease, then lying flat on the trouser, a hand. It was Alan's hand. She felt his eyes on her. She needed only to turn her head to meet them, but something inside her was panic-stricken. It was the stupid conventional idea that she had left him, that he had claims on her and was about to voice them, perhaps make a scene in Séverin's house, in the house of a man he had never met. She remained perfectly still. Beside her, touching her, that stranger sat breathing softly, a man who could not possibly understand the party, who was as bored as she by the bad singing, a man she had not seen for a month. In the darkness at her side, not speaking to her, perhaps not daring to speak to her: Alan. And for a second, she wanted him so fiercely that she moved her hand abruptly to her breast, as though she had been caught red-handed. At the same time, it dawned upon her that he alone, a stranger among people of her own sort, among her own friends, was near to her, not only physically but because of a past which now could be neither denied nor recovered, and which reduced to nothing the expression of gaiety and freedom she had worn ten minutes before.

'He sings badly,' whispered Alan, and she turned to him.

*

And then their eyes met, embarrassed and bewildered, denying and recognizing each other with a mixture of cordiality and mock surprise, rancour and panic, and all that each could see of the other was the glint of an eye, the outline of a too familiar face, the mute, excited twitching of a mouth. 'Where were you?' – 'Why did you come here?' – 'How could you leave me?' – 'What do you want now?' the questions brutally replacing the words of *Ole Man River* which, fortunately, was ending. Josée applauded with the others, reflecting on the strangeness of a gesture that consisted in clapping your hands together while someone looked straight at you – a ridiculous gesture that meant nothing to her (as she did not much like the singer). Nothing except the deliberate wish to identify herself with the other guests, her family, her compatriots, even though they had temporarily lapsed into bad taste – and by doing this to free herself from Alan, to confirm that she had resumed her own place in their life and that it would be hers from now on. At that moment, Séverin turned on the lights and she saw Alan's face clearly: so childlike, so disarmed, neither cruel nor predatory, it was the face of a decent, unhappy young man.

'What are you doing here?'

'I was looking for Bernard. He promised to find you for me.'

'Where did you get that awful tie?' she went on, and now that her first panic was over, a keen sense of happiness swept over her, obscuring all other thought.

'I bought it yesterday in the rue de Rivoli,' said Alan with a slight laugh.

They continued to talk without looking at one another, as though the singer had not stopped and some invisible show were taking place in the drawing-room.

'It was a mistake.'

'Yes.'

He said 'yes' in a whisper, and she could not tell if he was alluding to something else. Once more, she saw faces hovering round her, conversations were resumed, but she felt as remote from these people now as she had been close to them half an hour earlier. It all seemed like a play to her. A tipsy, giggling marionette went by and she recognized Elizabeth.

'Do you like Robin? Sings marvellously, doesn't he?'

Séverin leant over her, she casually introduced Alan who rose and shook hands cordially with his host.

'How do you do,' said Séverin – and he seemed embarrassed. 'Will you be in Paris for long?'

Alan mumbled something. She realized that they should leave as quickly as possible, even if it meant a scene once they were alone together – in any case, this agreeable party was turning into a horrible nightmare. She got up, kissed Séverin and left without looking back. Silently Alan followed her, opened the door, helped her on with her coat. Once outside, they took a few steps, irresolutely, before he could bring himself to take her arm.

'Where are you living?'

'In the rue du Bac. What about you? Oh, I know, at the Ritz.'

'May I see you home? I mean, to your door?'

'Of course.'

A light wind swept the street. They went off, stumbling a little. Josée's mind was a blank except for one thought: 'The shortest way is by the Boulevard Saint-Germain, but it will be terribly windy.' She watched her feet in a sort of stupor as she put them down one in front of the other, wondering vaguely when she had bought those shoes and where.

'How badly that fellow sang,' said Alan.

'Yes. We turn left here.'

They wheeled left like soldiers. Alan took his arm away, and for a second she felt completely lost.

'You see,' said Alan, 'all this is quite beyond me.'

'All what?'

She did not feel like talking. Above all, she did not want him to talk about themselves or their life. She wanted to go in. She was perfectly willing to go to bed with him, but she did not want to talk. Meanwhile, he leaned against a wall, lit a cigarette and continued to lean gazing into space.

'All this is quite beyond me,' he repeated. 'What am I doing here? Another thirty years to live, at most, and then what? What dirty trick is being played on us? What's the meaning of everything we do, or try to do? Some day, I'll be *nothing*. Can you understand it – nothing? I'll be torn away from this world, I'll be deprived of it and the earth will go on turning without me. How disgusting!'

She looked at him, hesitated, then leaned against the wall by him.

'It's absurd, you know, Josée. Whoever asked to live? It's as though we'd been invited to spend the week-end in a country house full of rotten planks and treacherous stair-cases, a house where we look in vain for the owner, God or whoever it may be. But nobody's there. And it's just a week-end, no more than a week-end. How can we be expected to have time enough to understand, to know, to love one another? What's this sinister joke? Nothing, do you realize? Some day, there'll be nothing. Darkness. Emptiness. Death.'

'What makes you talk like that?'

She shivered partly with cold and partly with sheer physical horror as she listened to his dreamy voice.

'Because I think of nothing else. But when you're with me, at night, when we're warm and together, then I don't give a damn. That's the only time when I don't give a damn. I don't give a damn about dying; my one fear is that you should die. What's far more important than anything else, than any other thought, is to feel your breath on me. I lie in wait like an animal. As soon as you wake up, I hide inside you, inside your mind, your consciousness. I fling myself on you, live on you. Oh, when I think that you took that plane without me, that it might have crashed! You're crazy! You had no right to do such a thing. Can you imagine: life without you?'

He corrected himself immediately:

'I mean: life if you were dead. I can understand that you don't want me any longer, I can understand that . . .'

He breathed in a puff of smoke, then suddenly detached himself from the wall.

'No. It's all beyond me, anyway. When I sat by you and you didn't see me for a few minutes, I felt doped or dead drunk. Yet, I haven't been drinking for a long time. It's really true, isn't it?'

He took her by the arm.

'I mean, there's something true, something real between us, isn't there?'

'Yes,' said Josée softly. She felt like leaning on him and, at the same time, wanted to escape from him. Yes, there was something real between them.

'I'm going,' said Alan, 'going back to my hotel. If I came as far as your door, I'd come in with you.'

He waited a second, but she said nothing.

'Will you come for me at the hotel tomorrow?' he asked in a whisper. 'You'll come very early? Promise?'

'Yes.'

She would have answered 'yes' to anything, and tears came into her eyes. For a moment, he leant towards her.

'Don't touch me,' she said.

She watched him go, he was running, and although her hotel was close at hand she hailed a taxi.

Infinitely sad, she went to bed at once, trembling with cold and with nerves. He had said exactly what he should have said, and by speaking in general terms of their own problem had shown her the stark realities of time and death, and he had persuaded her that the only means of eluding them, apart from religion, alcohol, or folly, was love. 'I love you, you're no longer certain of not loving me. I need you and what have you got to lose?' Yes, of course, he was right. But at the same time her feelings were like a wild animal, furious at being recaptured, and she desperately resented having allowed herself to be stirred. She had been so carefree, so gay, so alert when the party began, had felt such compassion for Elizabeth, had been so fascinated by Séverin and his little menagerie. Everything had become remote, meaningless, and unimportant as soon as she had noticed Alan's hand beside her. He cut her off from society. Not because she loved him too much, but because he disliked society and dragged her away with him into his own self-centred orbit. She was condemned to see him and him only because he could only see her. Exhausted, she turned her face to the wall and fell asleep suddenly.

*

It was fine, cold, and windy next morning. Leaving her hotel, she bitterly regretted having promised to go to the Ritz: she would have liked to sit outside the Deux-Magots or the Flore, meet old friends again, talk nonsense and drink tomato juice, as she used to. To see Alan at the Ritz seemed as artificial as an American film script, to have nothing to do with the air she breathed or her gentle pace as she ambled down the Boulevard Saint-Germain, quiet, peaceful, obedient to the traffic lights. She walked to the Place Vendôme, asked for Alan's room and only regained consciousness of herself, of Alan, of them both, when she opened the door.

He was in bed, shoulders bare, an old red scarf around his neck. The breakfast tray lay at the foot of the bed and she thought with some annoyance that he might at least have looked as though he expected her.

For she had left him of her own free will, and she was seeing him again to talk about a divorce. To be so scantily dressed seemed inappropriate to a discussion of this nature.

'You're looking wonderfully well,' he said. 'Sit down.'

There was an uncomfortable armchair that offered her the choice of either perching stiffly on the edge of the seat or sprawling. She sat down and perched.

'It's a good thing you aren't wearing a hat or carrying a handbag,' he remarked mockingly, 'or I'd take you for a social worker who's come to beg for my left-overs for the poor.'

'I've come to ask for a divorce,' she said dryly.

He burst out laughing.

'Don't look so fierce, anyway. You're like ... like a child. As a matter of fact, you've never left your childhood behind, it walks at your side, quiet, modest, demure, much like a double life. Your efforts to come closer to real life are pretty fruitless, aren't they, darling? Bernard and I were talking about it ...'

'I don't see how Bernard comes into this, but I'll tax him with it, in any case.'

'And you'll pull his ears for him, and he'll explain why you're more like a human being than anyone he knows.'

She sighed. Talking would be useless. There was nothing for it but to leave the hotel. However, Alan's flippancy, his smile worried her vaguely.

'Leave that armchair and come here,' he said. 'Are you afraid?'

'Afraid of what?'

She sat down on the bed. They were close to each other, and she could see his features soften very gradually, his eyes grow hazy. He stretched out his hand, took hers, laid it flat on a fold in the sheet.

'I want you,' he said. 'You know I do.'

'That's not the point, Alan.'

The red scarf touched her face, he pulled her down closer and all she could see then was the whiteness of the sheet and his sunburnt neck marked by a very definite crease.

'I want you,' he repeated.

'But listen, I'm all dressed, all made-up. I can scarcely breathe. Your enthusiasm is very flattering, but I've got to talk to you.'

Nevertheless, she found herself instinctively making a familiar caress and he panted a little as he lay close to her, fidgeting impatiently with her skirt. She gave in, at last, wondering if she were trying to get some sleep after a bad night or if she wanted the contact of a man's body close to hers again. Very soon, they were naked on the bed, hurried, exhausted, prey to the physical imagination that love can sometimes be, wondering with tears in their eyes what could have parted them so long, listening to, echoing, the body's pulsation – a pulsation so passionate and yet so inadequate – changing the Place Vendôme's quiet brightness into a syncopated series of lights and shadows and the carved wooden bed into a raft.

Afterwards they lay quiet for a moment, tenderly wiping the perspiration from each other's bodies. Already, she left everything to him.

'Tomorrow I'll look for an apartment for us,' he said finally.

She made no objection.

*

'I felt much more at home at Key Largo,' said Alan. 'But you didn't. For the time being, you need people round you. You want to see people, you believe in them. All right. Let's see people, your people, you'll point out the interesting ones to me. When you've had enough of it, we'll go back to somewhere quiet.'

She listened to him, her head bowed, with the sheepish expression of a frivolous woman as she answered:

'Good idea. And when we go back to somewhere quiet, you'll remember the names of my people, as you call them, you'll ask questions, you'll say: "What made you give Séverin chips on Friday, 9 October? Were you sleeping with him then?"'

*

He had thrown his glass on the floor in one of his rare fits of childishness, and the new housemaid had declared that if this sort of thing went on all the time she wouldn't be with them long, etc. In the end, their flat was very pleasant, although the rooms had sloping ceilings of a type that suggested Bohemian life as seen by Hollywood rather than an old part of Paris. Josée had provided three comfortable and relatively fine pieces of furniture, a piano, and a gigantic radiogram. They spent their first morning agreeably enough in a room that was empty except for a bed, lamp, and ashtray, listening to a magnificent recording of Bach that sent them back to sleep. The following day found them at antique dealers and the flea market. They also went to a few parties to which Josée brought Alan much as a cat lugs her kitten, delicately holding it between her teeth by the scruff of its neck, ready to clear out at the slightest sign of danger. Or at least, that was how Bernard described it. 'Only, cats behave like that out of love, not like you out of deference to public opinion,' he had added unkindly: 'for fear he might get tight or be disagreeable or make a scene.' But contrary to Bernard's expectation, Alan acted the part of a naïve, dazzled young American husband so ostentatiously that Josée was torn between rage and amusement.

'I'm so glad to have you as a guide, you know,' said Alan to the delighted Séverin. 'In America we're so far away from Europe, particularly from France, where things are so delicately refined, so subtle. I feel like an oaf among you, and I'm afraid of embarrassing Josée.'

This modest little speech, coupled with his good looks, won him every heart. People almost resented the fact that Josée did not make him feel more at ease. For her, hearing Alan pulling them all to pieces with cold ferocity each evening, it all became sad and funny at the same time, like a miscarriage of justice. However, not only Bernard but several of her friends had sometimes caught Alan laughing, had overheard his comments and regarded him with a mixture of distrust and liking that on the whole came fairly close to the less moderate feelings that divided Josée's heart – and this vaguely reassured her.

They had agreed, during the long and halting discussion that had followed the morning at the Ritz, a morning that neither felt strong enough to call anything but a reconcilia-tion – they had agreed to begin again on a new basis, an expression meant to sanction Josée's departure, their separation and their reunion. Not that either of them believed much in such terms, but since they were weary of their own vagaries, it was a sort of act of contrition jointly made to current social conventions and the beha-viour in their set. Yet another sentiment mingled with this weariness. They would not admit, neither of them, in their heart of hearts, that Josée's departure – painful for them both – the two rather distracted weeks spent apart and, above all, the party where they had met again which each remembered as extremely romantic (their surprise and terror, the coloured singer, the wind) – no, they would not admit that all this did not correspond to a decision. In fact, for Alan, it amounted to: 'You admit that I should share the whole of your life,' and for Josée: 'You admit that you aren't the whole of life.' But they did not say that, but simply: 'We're free, we're mixing with people, we're trying to mix with them as a couple.'

The drawback was that things lost their savour. Alan's eyes followed her wherever she went, judging whomever she talked to. She thought that she could hear a little machine working inside him, unceasingly busy with cross-checks, hypotheses, calculations, of which she would only be given a faint echo in the evening – as he feared she might run away again – but of which she was ever conscious, to such a degree that she would turn round suddenly to catch him in the act of spying on her, as he almost always was. Apart from this, there was bed and love-making, and she wondered that it could still exist and survive her weariness. At night together they recaptured their former emotion, the haste and breathlessness of love, but it turned into mutual distrust as soon as they wakened in the morning. No doubt it was not for physical love alone that she remained with him, but would she have stayed without it?

Meanwhile, they gradually settled down to their new life: interminable mornings, light luncheons, afternoons devoted to shopping or to museums, dinners with Josée's old friends. Alan didn't work, of course. They led the life of tourists, and this greatly contributed to Josée's feeling of impermanency, of unreality, a feeling that Alan fostered as he waited complacently for the time when she could bear it no longer and he could take her somewhere else. Meanwhile, he was pleasant, with the kind of indulgent pleasantness which one reserves for other people's whims. Only in this case, and she knew it, the whim was her own life.

They saw a great deal of Bernard. He understood the game they were playing and tried by every means to help Josée, give her back the Paris she loved, re-create its charm, bring her into contact with people. But more often he felt as though he were struggling with a deaf mute, desperately intent on taking part in a conversation, than assisting a free young woman, who should have been able to cope for herself. He could see her eyes glance aside suddenly, search the drawing-room, meet Alan's and then return to him anxiously, filled with a sort of impotent rage. He ended by thinking that her sole act of independence had been her absurd tumble with the shark fisherman. When he told her this one day, she turned her head away evasively.

'It's as though you led a double life,' he said, 'as though you were shadowed by another life so close to childhood that you can't tear yourself away from it, a life where you're not responsible and yet punished, always tied to people who judge you and to whom you have given a right to judge you, simply because you have the power to make them suffer.'

She shook her head absently. They were at Séverin's house again that evening and in such a crowd that they could talk quietly together, at last.

'That's what Alan was saying the other day! So you see eye to eye. But what else have you to offer me?' she asked.

'I ...?' He hesitated to say 'everything' because it sounded literary. 'I? This has nothing to do with me. The point is that you're a prisoner and unhappy. And that's not like you.'

'What is like me?'

'Anything you aren't forced to submit to. Just because he loves you in an obnoxious way, you take that for something positive. It isn't.'

She took a cigarette and smiled as she used the lighter he held out.

'I'll tell you how it is: Alan is convinced that each human being wallows in the mud he was born in and that nothing can drag him out of it – particularly not the vague notions and incomprehensible sentences he brings himself to make or pronounce daily. In this sense Alan himself can't be touched or reached.'

'What about you?'

She leaned against the wall, suddenly relaxed, talking so low that he was obliged to bend forward to hear her:

'Well, I don't believe in such emptiness. That kind of pathos bores me stiff. No one gets drowned. I believe that every man sketches his own life in bold, sweeping strokes, in a splendid assertive manner. I don't respond to half-tones. I only see lyrical emotions everywhere, even if they go by the name of boredom, love, depression, or laziness. In fact . . .'

She took Bernard's hand, squeezed it, and he realized that she had completely forgotten Alan's inquisitive glances for a minute.

'In fact, I don't believe that we're just numbers. We're more like live animals, lyrical live animals.'

He pressed her hand between his, kept it. She did not draw it away. He felt like kissing, hugging, comforting her. 'My sweet little animal,' he whispered, 'my lyrical little animal,' and she gently moved away from the wall and quietly kissed him, right in a crowd of people. 'If that fool comes bawling up, if that obsessed husband of hers interferes, I'll brain him,' thought Bernard, closing his eyes. But her lips had already left his and he found that you can

kiss someone on the mouth in the midst of a party without anyone being the wiser.

Josée left him at once. She had no idea why she had kissed him, but felt no embarrassment whatever. There was something irresistible in the look he gave her, such an expression of tenderness, of acceptance, that everything else had slipped out of her mind. She was married to Alan and Bernard to Nicole, she was not in love with him, yet she had perhaps never felt closer to anyone than to him at that moment. It seemed as though she could not have borne Alan to comment on it, supposing by chance he had seen them, but at the same time she knew very well that he had not. The sight of that kiss would have been so intolerable to him that something must have prevented his witnessing it. 'I'm beginning to believe in fate,' she thought, and laughed.

'I've been looking for you,' said Alan. 'Just imagine, I've met a fellow I used to study painting with at university. He lives here. I've a good mind to take it up again with him.'

'So you paint?' She was dumbfounded.

'I liked it immensely, when I was eighteen. And then, it's an occupation, isn't it? The apartment is fitted up and furnished and I don't see how I'll fill in my time, as I'm not very practical-minded.'

There was more enthusiasm than irony in his voice.

'Don't worry,' he said, taking her by the shoulders and clasping her tightly to him, 'I won't ask you to mix colours for me, you can wander around with those old friends of yours or, better still, alone . . .'

'Have you talent?'

'Maybe this will save me,' she thought, 'maybe he'll become interested in something that isn't us two.' At the same time, she felt annoyed with herself for thinking so selfishly.

'I don't really think so, but I can draw pretty well. I'll begin tomorrow. The empty room at the back of the flat will do.'

'It's dark, you won't see a thing there.'

'I don't even know how to paint what I see,' he said, and burst out laughing. 'I'll send my first picture to my mother and she'll show it to the family psychiatrist – he'll certainly be amused.'

She looked at him hesitantly. He let go of her.

'Aren't you pleased? I thought you'd like me to do something on my own.'

'I'm very pleased,' she answered. 'It will do you a world of good.'

At times, Alan projected on to her the reactions of his mother. And, in point of fact, Josée really came very near to having a few of them.

*

'How are you getting on?'

She opened the door, thrust her head into the room. Alan wore an elegant dark blue suit even to paint in and had greeted with horror Séverin's suggestion that artists should wear sweaters and corduroy trousers. As a matter of fact, the back room did not have much of the atmosphere of a studio. Simply an easel a little way from the window, a table covered with a neat array of tubes, a few blank canvases on a shelf, and, in the middle of the room, seated on a comfortable armchair, a well-dressed young man, casually smoking. He looked as if he were waiting for inspiration. Nevertheless, he had spent every afternoon there for the past two weeks, leaving his work without a trace of fatigue, in excellent spirits and spotlessly clean. Josée felt perplexed, but, whether all this was a game or not, she had four hours to herself every day and that was a great thing.

'I'm getting on all right. What have you been doing?'

'Nothing. I've been strolling about.'

That was the truth. After lunch, she went off in the car, driving slowly through the streets and stopping when she felt like it. She had discovered a square that she particularly liked because of a romantic-looking tree, and often spent an hour there without leaving the car, looking at occasional passers-by and the wind stirring in the leafless wintry branches. She would daydream, smoke, listen to the radio sometimes, motionless, dead to herself, filled with the sweetest enjoyment. She dared not tell Alan of all this, it might have made him even more jealous than if she had been with someone. However, she had no desire to see anyone. Later, she would leave the square, always driving slowly and at random. The afternoon gradually came to an end and the necessity of returning to Alan began to weigh on her, accompanied by a sense of relief, as though he were the only tie that bound her to life. Sleeping, dreaming . . . she would have liked to spend her life on a beach staring at the sea, or in the country breathing in the smell of grass, or in a corner of her square, a life to dream away in solitude, while time remained as motionless as her own thoughts.

'When will you show me something?'

'In a week, perhaps. Why do you laugh?'

'Because you look so much like someone at a polite tea party. One always hears about artists struggling to paint.'

'I don't know about struggling, but it's quite true I can't stand getting my hands dirty, but it's difficult not to when you paint. I'm thirsty, aren't you?'

'Very. While you remove that speck of crimson lake from your forefinger, I'll mix you a dry Martini. That's the artist's wife for you, practical and helpful.'

'I wish you would pose for me.'

She pretended not to hear and quickly closed the door

behind her. He joined her later, but did not repeat his last remark. He drank less since he had taken up painting, and even tried to make himself at home in the flat, as though he really lived there.

'Where did you go?'

'Nowhere special. I had a cup of tea in a little square near the Porte d'Orléans.'

'Alone?'

'Yes.'

He smiled. She looked closely at him. He gave a little laugh.

'I suppose you don't believe me?'

'Oh yes, I do.'

She almost asked: 'Why?' but refrained. But she was astonished by his apparent lack of curiosity. She got up.

'I'm very glad, that you believe me, I mean.'

She spoke tenderly. He blushed and his voice rose.

'You're glad that my morbid jealousy is better. You're glad that my little mind is no longer so one-track. You're glad that I have an occupation at last, like any man worthy of the name, even if it amounts to smearing paint on canvas, aren't you?'

She dropped into an armchair without answering. A scene was about to begin.

' "My husband has turned into a real husband at last, he gives me four hours of peace a day." That's what you think to yourself. "He messes up canvases that some poor chap with twice the talent probably can't afford to buy, but who cares so long as he leaves me alone?" Isn't that it?'

'I'm glad you're developing a social conscience at last. Anyway, you aren't the only one to daub, if that's all you're capable of doing.'

'I don't just daub. I do a bit better than that. It's as good an occupation as sitting for hours in a car, staring at a square.'

'I'm not criticizing you,' she said, then stopped. 'How do you know that I . . . that . . . my square . . .?'

'I have you followed,' he replied. 'What do you think?'

She looked at him, thunderstruck. What she felt was not anger but a dreadful calm, for nothing had changed. Life went on as usual.

'You have me followed? All the afternoon? Do you really paint?'

She burst out laughing. He had become quite pale. Seizing her by the arm, he dragged her still spluttering with laughter into the back room. 'That poor detective,' she said, 'how bored he must be!'

'Here's my first picture.'

He turned a canvas face up. Although Josée knew very little about painting, this one struck her as not at all bad, and she stopped laughing.

'It's good, you know.'

He flung the picture back against the wall and eyed it dubiously for a moment.

'What do you think about when you sit alone in the car for hours? Who do you think about? Do tell me, *please*.'

He clasped her tightly in his arms. She was filled with both disgust and pity.

'Why do you have me followed? Don't you know that it's simply not done any more and it's very bad manners. That poor man must hate my square.'

She felt herself about to laugh again, and bit her lip.

'Tell me what you think about.'

'I think about . . . I don't know. Honestly, I don't know what I think about. About that tree, about you, about people, about summer . . .'

'But just what do you think exactly . . .?'

She freed herself brusquely, she no longer had the slightest desire to laugh.

'Let me go. You look – I don't know how to express it –

you look obscene when you cross-question me like that. I don't think about anything, do you hear? Not a single thing!'

She slammed the door and ran out of the house. When she returned an hour later in a calmer frame of mind she found him dead drunk.

*

They were all three in the little drawing-room, at last provided with a sofa and a couple of armchairs. Josée lay on the sofa, the two men looking down at her as they talked. It was late afternoon.

'So you see,' said Bernard, 'she's madly in love with you, my dear Alan.'

'That's rather a good thing,' said Josée carelessly, 'she's been nasty enough to a few people in her time.'

'I can't place her,' said Alan, looking appalled.

'Laura Dort? She was at dinner at Séverin's about ten days ago. She's fifty or thereabouts, used to be very beautiful, still isn't bad now. She often has people in on Thursday.'

'Fifty? That's a bit of an exaggeration, Josée. She can't be more than forty and she's all right, very much so.'

'Well anyway, I've no time for her,' said Alan. 'I don't suppose you'd be jealous about that, would you?'

'Well . . .' said Josée smiling. 'You never can tell! In any case, it would be a change.'

Bernard burst out laughing. In the vain hope of diminishing Alan's jealousy, they had adopted the habit of joking about it, as though it were simply eccentricity. Alan always laughed too, though his attitude was really quite unchanged, which the other two found rather disconcerting.

'Now will you go and see her after dinner or not? I must be off at once.'

'We'll think it over,' said Alan. 'Oh, we'll go and see a thriller first and then join you afterwards.'

When Bernard left, they discussed Laura Dort for a moment. Josée knew her very well. She had an accommodating husband in business and a morbid passion for the same kind of society as Séverin, she had had two or three well-connected lovers without causing too much scandal, and had tormented several others with little regard for their feelings. She was the kind of woman who always seems to be on the alert, and Josée usually became silent in her presence. But from sheer curiosity she spoke rather charitably about her to Alan. Furthermore, she was intelligent, often entertaining, and Josée had a certain respect for her.

They reached her house at midnight, in a good humour after an atrocious film, and Laura Dort gave them an effusive reception. She was tall, red-headed, with generous curves and a cat-like face. Josée was surprised to find that she felt vaguely apprehensive. After the introductions had been performed in the style of: 'You all remember Josée?' and 'This is Alan Ash,' Alan started at once playing the dazzled American and was immediately pounced upon. Josée, seeing that Bernard was talking to someone, joined a friend she had known 'before'. Bernard came up to her a little later.

'It seems to be going off very well.'

'What?'

'Laura and Alan. Look.'

They were standing at the other end of the drawing-room, Laura staring at Alan with a curious expression on her face as he smilingly told her about the film he and Josée had just seen. Josée whistled to herself.

'Did you see her expression?'

'That's called passion. Passion as expressed by Laura Dort. Love at first sight, darling.'

'Poor thing . . .' said Josée.

'Don't look so confident, it gets on my nerves. And if you want my advice, act jealous, it will give you a breathing space. Or really be jealous, one never knows . . .'

She smiled. It was difficult to feel relieved at the idea of abandoning Alan to Laura's somewhat tarnished embrace. She would have preferred him to concentrate on painting. She could visualize leaving him even less than continuing to stay with him. Ever since her return to Paris she felt as though she had been walking on a tightrope, living in a sort of armed neutrality as far removed from happiness as from the despair she had experienced at Key Largo.

'A pretty half-baked solution,' she murmured to herself.

'They're often the best,' said Bernard, before adding hesitantly: 'If I haven't misunderstood things, you still want to get rid of him? Without making a drama of it. Am I right?'

'I think so,' she replied. 'I'm no longer very sure what I want, other than peace.'

'You mean, somebody else. But you'll never find anyone else as long as he's around. You realize that, don't you?'

'I'm not very sure of what *you* want,' thought Josée, but said nothing. Alan came up to her, followed by Laura. 'Mature women don't suit him,' she thought, 'he's too attractive, they make him look like a gigolo.'

'I've been imploring your husband to spend a week-end at Vaux where I have a house. He looks as though he might accept, but his answer depends on you. I'm sure you're as fond of the country as ever, aren't you?'

'Who is she alluding to?' thought Josée rapidly. 'Oh yes, I stayed at her house with Marc, four years ago.' She smiled.

'I adore the country. I'd love to come.'

'It will do her good,' said Alan as he turned to Laura, 'she's looking pale these days.'

'At her age, one should always look well,' said Laura lightly.

She took Alan's arm and carried him off. Bernard began to laugh.

'That's an old ploy. "Josée is only a child, my dear Alan, now we grown-ups, etc." You'll only have a hot-water bottle in your bed at Vaux and you'll be made to play Old Maid with Monsieur Dort.'

'I think I'll probably enjoy myself,' said Josée. 'I adore cards and hot-water bottles and old gentlemen. And other women's treachery is always fun.'

Once they were home, Alan remarked pompously that Laura was extremely civilized and knew how to entertain.

'How strange,' said Josée, 'that among all the people I've introduced you to, and who are often admittedly a little crazy, you should have a good opinion of the only one who has no major virtues.'

'What are the major virtues?'

He was in a good mood. Laura must have showered him with compliments, and Josée thought herself very ingenuous not to have realized that he liked them. A healthy dose of masculine vanity must be lurking even in a man as detached as Alan.

'The major virtues . . .? I don't really know. A sense of humour, perhaps, and unselfishness. She has neither.'

'Nor have I. But then, I'm American.'

'And that's certainly what she likes about you. Remember to take your tartan dressing-gown to wear at breakfast. You look like a young cowboy in it, she'll be thrilled.'

He turned to her.

'If this week-end bores you, we don't have to go, you know.'

He seemed delighted. 'I ought to make a scene and act jealous,' thought Josée. 'Bernard is right.' She removed her make-up and went to bed, looking vexed. 'I'd never manage to do it on the same scale as Alan,' she thought as she fell asleep and smiled to herself in the darkness.

*

The house at Vaux was a long farmhouse, turned into an English country place by a smart decorator, furnished with vast leather sofas and curtains of the coarse folk-weave which had become so fashionable and so expensive. They arrived at five, were taken for a long walk on the estate – 'My real refuge,' Laura had said gravely, tossing back her red hair as they strolled under the trees. They had eaten the inevitable boiled eggs – 'I can swear they were laid this very day,' Laura had said, shaking her bright hair at the guests – and at that moment they were sampling the local brandy – 'It's as good as any whisky in the world,' Laura was saying, as she made her red head glint and glimmer in the firelight. Settling on the sofa, Josée wondered how long their hostess would be able to remain squatting in front of the hearth like Gigi, holding out her painted nails and ecstatic face to the flaming logs. The guests, apart from Josée and Alan, were a taciturn young painter, two chattering young women and – apparently – Laura's husband. He was small and thin, with bespectacled blue eyes, and seemed to hesitate each time he took a cigarette from a *Hermès* box. Alan, very much at ease, talked about New York with one of the young women, and Josée, yawning a little, decided to go to the next room, the library. 'Everyone must feel at home here,' Laura had declared. 'I loathe hostesses who force themselves on their guests.' Taking her at her word, Josée ransacked the bookshelves laden with magnificent editions of Le Sage and of Voltaire's *Letters*, both carefully dusted – and plunged into a detective story. Ten minutes later, she put the book down and closed her eyes. Five years earlier, she had been in this very room with her particular set and her current boy friend; they

79

had driven rather fast from Paris, four or five of them piled into Marc's old MG, for in those days they always went about in a gang. They had spent the whole night talking and laughing, and Marc was sulky because he would rather have taken her off to bed. What good friends they were, jealous and tender, they never imagined then that life might separate them and that some day anything could appear more important than their laughter and their confidence in one another. She wondered why these memories were both so gay and so painful, weighing on her like a threat, and suddenly she got up from her armchair. At that moment she noticed Laura's husband lying on a sofa. He saw her, too, and started. He had not said a single word that evening except for one short, quick observation when Alan declared his complete indifference towards politics. 'One hasn't grown up until one starts to take an interest in the world around one,' a sentence rapidly drowned in the general hum of conversation. She gave him a smile and motioned to him to stay where he was.

'I didn't know you were here,' he mumbled. 'Will you have a drink?'

She shook her head.

'I couldn't stand the smoke in the next room. Is it you who read Le Sage?'

He smiled and shrugged his shoulders.

'The decorator put them there, the bindings are supposed to be very fine. Perhaps one winter evening, with a good pipe and a faithful dog at my knee, I may get round to reading them. I haven't had time.'

'Too much work?'

'Yes. I add up figures all day, I calculate, I make telephone calls. It's wonderful to have this refuge in the country where we can relax after the frenzied life in the city.'

'Yes, Laura said that Vaux was her only refuge.'

'Yes?'

There was something so sarcastic about his 'yes' that she burst out laughing.

'Here, we have time to think about ourselves,' he repeated like a lesson, 'to watch time go by. There are fields where people never lie down, flowers that the gardener cuts, the smell of earth that can make you melancholy in autumn.'

She sat down by him. His face was that of a small boy of sixty, chubby and wrinkled at the same time. His eyes sparkled behind his glasses.

'Don't take any notice of what I say, I must have had too much to drink. Whenever my wife entertains, I drink too much brandy to take away the taste of those damned eggs our hens lay every day. Our hens come from Yorkshire, you see. Apparently all the best hens do.'

'He's very tight or very unhappy,' thought Josée, 'or else he has a certain wit.' She instinctively preferred the last explanation.

'Do Laura's guests bore you very much?'

'Not in the least. I'm seldom here. I have to travel a good deal. For instance, it's five years since I first heard about you, and yet we've never met. A great pity, because you're very attractive.'

He ended his last sentence with a little nod of the head and added hurriedly:

'Your husband is very good-looking too. Your children must be lovely.'

'I have no children.'

'But you will and they'll be very beautiful.'

'My husband doesn't want children,' said Josée abruptly.

There was a moment of silence. She regretted both her answer and the over-hasty confidence that he had inspired.

'He's afraid you'd prefer them to him,' he said firmly.

'What makes you say that?'

'It's quite obvious. He looks only at you, just as my wife looks only at him and just as you look only into space.'

'A pretty trio,' she said dryly.

'A pretty quartet if you admit that I look only at the Stock Exchange prices.'

They stared at each other and could not help laughing.

'And you couldn't care less?' asked Josée.

'I've reached the happy age when you can only care for people who do you good. I don't mean to say that doesn't make you suffer. I mean people who respect your integrity. You'll see, it will happen to you some day. You must excuse me, my brandy glass is empty.'

He rose and she followed him into the drawing-room. They paused on the threshold. Alan sat at Laura's feet and she was looking down at him so tenderly, so avidly, that Josée shrank back. Alan raised his eyes and gave her a knowing wink that made her blush. For an instant she feared that Dort might have intercepted the wink, but he was already across the room on his way to the bar. In any case, she did not wish to be involved in Alan's little games.

She told him so when they had gone up to bed. He paced up and down the room, describing to her with smug brutality the forms which Laura's interest in him had taken.

'I don't care for your brand of fun. People shouldn't be made fun of like that, no matter who they are.'

He stopped walking about.

'You didn't always think that. You used to come here fairly often in the old days.'

'Sometimes.'

'Who with?'

'With friends.'

'With one or several friends?'

'I said *friends*.'

'You've never told me anything about this house. You've

told me stories about the seaside, the mountains, the town, never about the country. Why?'

She buried her head in the pillow. When she felt some difficulty in breathing, she raised it cautiously. Alan was looking intently at her.

'Don't worry, I'll find out.'

'From Laura?'

'Who do you think I am? From you, my sweet, and soon.'

This turned out to be truer than he imagined.

*

There was certainly something strange in Laura's behaviour; something challenging about it that came near to defiance. When Josée came down to breakfast, before her husband, Laura welcomed her loudly and warmly and then began praising Alan to the skies.

'He's still asleep? He's still a child really, and must need a lot of sleep. What's so charming in these young Americans is that you feel as though they'd just been born the second you meet them. Do you want some coffee?'

'No, tea.'

'Wasn't that your impression when you met Alan? That he had no past? That there hadn't been any women in his life before you?'

'Not exactly,' said Josée rather drowsily.

'The only drawback,' continued Laura without noticing the interruption, 'is that they imagine the rest of the world are like them. Whereas, we Europeans . . .'

Josée had not listened to what followed. She had raised her eyes a moment and then reached out for a slice of toast. And now, after a walk which lasted most of the morning and during which Laura had never let go of Alan's arm, dragging him well ahead of the other guests who were stunned by so much fresh air, Josée remembered her

83

hostess's words and wondered mildly what she was getting at. As it was sunny, they all sat in deck-chairs in front of the house drinking fruit juice. Josée was thinking of what Jean-Pierre Dort had said: . . . 'fields where people never lie down,' when Laura got up in a decidedly excited mood.

'I'm going to take Alan away from you. I want to show him that wonderful attic of mine before lunch.'

As she said this she smiled at Josée who smiled back.

'I won't suggest your coming with us, Josée, I think you already know it.'

Josée made an evasive gesture. It was in that attic, five years before, that Laura had found her with Marc, in a compromising situation. At the time they had all joked a lot about that charming attic. So Laura imagined that she could frighten her, did she? She was so angry that she turned quite pale, and the young painter broke his silence to offer her a glass of port with an air of complicity that put the finishing touch to her rage.

'Do you mean the attic where I slept with Marc?' she asked calmly.

A horrified silence ensued. Josée turned to Alan.

'I don't know if I ever told you about it. A chap called Marc, when I was twenty. Laura can give you the details.'

A young woman burst out laughing, no doubt because it was impossible to say anything and the young painter followed suit.

'Who hasn't made merry in this house!' he said gaily. 'It's such a hospitable house.'

'Your expression seems a trifle out of place,' said Laura furiously. 'And thank God I don't know the details of Josée's escapades.'

'My wife's past escapades are her own business,' said Alan tenderly, as he bent to kiss Josée's hair.

'He's going to bite me,' she thought suddenly and, foreseeing all the questions and fits of rage that her outburst

84

would provoke, closed her eyes, already exhausted. She was really too stupid. Alan smiled at her, looking so pleased that he must surely be mad or wildly neurotic. She must leave him before something dreadful happened, before it was too late. But she did not budge from her seat. It was the same at the cinema: she could never leave before the end.

Marc was their only topic of conversation for the next two months. How had she met Marc, what did she like about him, and how long did it last? All her efforts to reduce him into an insignificant incident were useless: even disparagement seemed to fire Alan's imagination. For after all, if he was as unimportant as she claimed there must have been something else, something else that she could not say. Things were so bad that she seized every opportunity that would take them out in the evening, and keep them out until they were both exhausted, simply to put off the moment when raising himself on his elbows, he would say: 'It was better with him, wasn't it?' And then would come a flood of questions always precise, sometimes crude, that she detested. At the end of two months of this, her face was puffy with alcohol, and there were dark circles round her eyes. Suddenly she rebelled. She went to bed before ten, did physical jerks and met Alan's threats and entreaties with obstinate silence. Every one of his remarks contained a trap and more than once she found herself hating him.

Laura Dort was now always with them. They spent almost every evening together, usually at her house, for she gave very agreeable dinners, after which Alan would take her round the night-clubs, until by dawn she was haggard, but delighted, and looked a good ten years older. She frequently spent the afternoon with them and had developed a great enthusiasm for Alan's pictures. She went about telling everyone what a charming young couple they were and how much younger she felt in their company.

Josée ran away as soon as Laura appeared, leaving her to wander between the drawing-room and the studio where Alan, visibly charmed to have an audience, held forth extravagantly. When she came back, she would find them sunk in armchairs, drinking the first of their evening cocktails. Now that she no longer drank, she had the greatest difficulty in following their conversation. She noted with a sidelong glance the fresh lines in Laura's face, the puffiness under her eyes and the diabolical solicitude with which Alan kept refilling her glass. He never ceased to be charmingly attentive to her, inquiring into the minutest detail of her life and dancing with her for hours on end. Josée had not the slightest idea what he was up to.

Coming home a little late one evening, she found Bernard sitting between Laura and Alan. He was just back from abroad, and although she threw her arms round his neck he continued to look very gloomy. As soon as Laura had gone, he turned to Josée.

'What are you two playing at?'

Josée raised her eyebrows.

'What are we playing at?'

'Yes. You and Alan. What are you trying to do to that poor Laura?'

'Nothing as far as I'm concerned. You'd better ask Alan.'

The latter smiled, but Bernard did not turn in his direction.

'I'm asking you, Josée. You always used to be kind. What's the idea of making that wretched woman completely ridiculous? Everyone is laughing at her. Don't tell me you don't know.'

'I didn't know,' said Josée with annoyance. 'Anyway, I've had nothing to do with it.'

'Yes you have, in that you let that little sadist wreck her life, fill her up with drink and fantastic ideas.'

Alan whistled with admiration.

'Little sadist . . . What will you call me next?'

'Why do you let Laura believe that you are in love with her or on the verge of it? Why have you put her in such a ludicrous position? Who are you getting even with by means of her?'

'I'm not getting even with anyone. I'm having a little fun.'

Alan winked. Bernard was furious. Josée remembered that there had been a great deal of talk about a liaison between Laura and Bernard in the good old days of Vaux.

'Your idea of fun is just what one would expect from someone like you. The fun of an over-rich narcissistic little twerp. You two lead an idiotic life, you because of God knows what tiresome complex, Josée through sheer spinelessness, which is much worse.'

'You always come back in a charming mood,' said Josée. 'What was your trip like?'

'When are you going to make up your mind to leave this character?'

Alan got up, aimed a punch at him, and there was a fight, which, since they were equally incompetent, was both clumsy and unbecoming. Nevertheless they were heated enough for Alan's nose to start bleeding when it collided with Bernard's elbow. The table covered with bottles was overturned, gin flooded the carpet, glasses rolled under the chairs, and Josée yelled at them to stop. They looked at each other like idiots with their hair all over the place, and Alan took out a handkerchief to wipe his nose.

'Let's sit down,' said Josée. 'What were we talking about?'

'You must forgive me, Josée,' said Bernard. 'Laura is an old friend, even if she does get on my nerves, and she's been very generous to lots of people. But I never thought I'd have to defend her honour, all the same.'

'I'm bleeding like a pig,' said Alan. 'If I'd known I'd

have to fight all of Josée's beaux, I'd have taken a course with the Marines before marrying her.'

He began to laugh.

'Bernard, did you ever know someone called Marc something or other?'

'No,' replied Bernard firmly. 'You've asked me that already. And it has nothing to do with Laura.'

'I don't wish Laura any harm. I have no designs on her money or her virtue. Laura's an artist, that's all. And as it happens, she's going to sponsor my exhibition.'

'Your exhibition?' asked Josée.

'Certainly. She brought an art critic here yesterday. It seems my pictures are very good. I'm showing them in a month's time. So I hope to prove that I'm not such a parasite as your friend claims, dear Josée.'

'Which critic was it?' asked Josée.

'I think his name was Daumier.'

'He's an excellent critic,' said Bernard. 'Congratulations. I hope you aren't angry with me?'

He looked icy. Still bewildered, Josée saw him to the door.

'What do you think of this?'

'My opinion hasn't changed,' he said angrily. 'He wouldn't give you a moment's peace, even if he became prime minister. So you can imagine how much less as a painter! I should never have helped him to find you.'

'Why do you say that? On account of Laura?'

'Yes, among other things. I used to think him slightly mad but nice. He's not nice and he's raving mad.'

'Aren't you exaggerating?' she said.

They stood on the landing in the dark and he held her by the wrist.

'He'll destroy you. Don't fool yourself. Escape while you still can.'

She tried to protest, but he was already on his way down.

Pensively, she went back to the drawing-room. Alan came up to her and took her in his arms.

'What a business . . . My nose hurts horribly. Are you pleased about my show?'

She spent the evening applying compresses and making light-hearted plans with him. He was like a helpless child who had taken up painting only to please her. He fell asleep in her arms, and for a long time she fondly watched him sleeping.

During the night she woke, bathed in perspiration. Bernard's remarks had struck home. She had dreamt that Laura lay disfigured on the lawn at Vaux. And although Josée cried out for help, people went by her, unseeing. She ran from one to the other, showing them Laura, but they looked annoyed and said: 'There's nothing wrong.' Alan sat smiling in an armchair. Josée left her bed, staggered to the bathroom, drank two huge glasses of water, thinking she could never tire of feeling the pure, icy liquid run down her throat. Alan grunted faintly, and she glanced at him. In the beam of light coming from the bathroom, he seemed half dead, lying back in the armchair, his handsome face disfigured by his swollen nose. She smiled. It was five o'clock and she no longer felt in the least sleepy. Catching up a dressing-gown, she tiptoed from the room.

In the drawing-room the first sickly light of dawn, half frightening, half reassuring, could just be discerned. She drew an armchair to the window and sat down. The street was deserted, the air clean and fresh. Suddenly, she remembered her return trip from New York. She had left at noon, and when she reached Paris six hours later, it was midnight. Within a single half hour, she had seen the dazzling morning sun go down, turn red and disappear, while evening shadows seemed to launch an attack against the plane, filing by the port-holes in ranks of blue, mauve, and finally black clouds. In the space of a moment she had passed into night. She experienced a strange desire to bathe in that sea of clouds, that blend of air, wind, and water that she imagined so light and soft against her skin, as enveloping as the memories of childhood. There was something incredible about these sky-scapes, something that reduced your life to an idiotic dream 'full of sound and fury', a dream achieved at the expense of this romantic serenity that filled the eyes with joy and should have been the true, the real life. To be alone, alone and lying on a beach, letting time go by as she felt it passing now, here in this empty room where the dawn hesitated to intrude. To escape from life, from what others called life, escape from all feelings, from her own virtues and from her own vices, to be nothing more than a transitory breath on the millionth part of one of the billions of galaxies. She stretched, cracked the joints of her arms, stood still. How many times had Alan or Bernard or Laura experienced this uncommunicable sensation? – how many times had they attempted to put it into words that immediately disfigured it? These frail collections of bone, blood, and grey matter that snatched little joys and little sorrows from one another before disappearing . . . she smiled. She knew only too well how useless it was to confront the problems of their life with a wiser infinite. Day was about to break, strident, demanding of words and gestures.

*

'Congratulations, Mr Ash. There's something new about your painting, a . . .'

The stranger swept his arm in a wide curve, groping for the word he had in mind, found it:

'A science. That's it, a fresh science of art. Most impressive.'

Alan smiled, bowed. He seemed very moved, the exhibition was a great success. Conducted in a masterly fashion by Laura, the publicity had been striking. The newspapers talked about strength, invention, depth. The women looked at Alan. People were surprised not to have heard before of the young American who had come to Paris in search of inspiration. It was whispered that he had arrived on a cargo boat as a coal-trimmer. All this would have amused Josée vastly if, during the three weeks preceding the show, Alan had not seemed so upset. They had spent them without leaving their flat, Alan groaning with apprehension, getting up at night to look at his pictures and making her get up too, talking about his paint brushes as though his life depended on them, frightening even Laura by his heart-searchings and wrestlings with his conscience, forcing Josée to be constantly with him either as mother, mistress, or critic. But she felt happy. He was interested in something other than himself, he talked about his work with respect and passion. He had created something. Suddenly their life together became possible once more, a life in which he needed her, of course, but as a man needs a woman. He had something else now. And so Josée serenely watched Laura Dort play the muse and Alan gradually straighten up mentally, relax, and become slightly superior: she preferred talking about Van Dyck to talking about Marc. She whispered this to Séverin when he had threaded his way towards her, dressed in black corduroy.

'I can sympathize,' he said smiling, 'he's driven me round the bend with his questions. Do you know that almost everything has been sold?'

'Yes. What do you think of it?'

'Absolutely wonderful. It makes me think of . . . er . . .'

'Don't strain yourself,' said Josée. 'I'm sure you don't know a thing about it.'

'Very true. Are we dining with Laura afterwards? Just look at her, you'd think she'd done it all.'

'She's delighted,' said Josée, who felt enormously charitable towards Laura. 'And really she has helped him a lot.'

'That's what everybody is saying,' Séverin continued quickly. 'You're going to be in for a lot of spiteful comments.'

'I like playing that kind of role,' replied Josée with a shrug.

'So long as people leave you in peace?'

They burst out laughing. Alan turned, frowning, then smiled when he saw Séverin.

'How nice of you to come. What do you think of the show?'

'Terrific,' said Séverin.

'That seems to be the general opinion,' said Alan with a self-satisfied little laugh, and turned to a new admirer.

Séverin cleared his throat, a little embarrassed, and Josée blushed.

'If he begins taking himself for Picasso . . .'

'It's better than taking himself for Othello, my sweet.'

He whisked her away with him. They left the gallery and sat outside a café. The air was soft, the sun was setting behind the Invalides, and Séverin chattered while Josée half-listened. She recalled Alan's tense face only ten days earlier: 'Do you think they're good? Do you think they amount to anything? Do tell me what you really think.' And then his expression, a few minutes ago: 'That seems to be the general opinion.' The change had been a little too sudden, usually Alan was too intelligent and above all too free from vanity.

'You aren't listening to me, are you?'

'Indeed I am, Séverin.'

He banged on the table with his fist.

'No, you're not. You've never listened to me since you came back. You don't listen to anyone, you always seem to be on the look out. The pair of you are like a couple of ghosts. I suppose you realize it?'

'Yes.'

'That's the main thing.'

Surprised by his serious tone, she turned to him, then started angrily.

'You talk just like Bernard. Aren't you a little too much interested in our private life?'

'Bernard ought to mind his own business and so should I. But he's fond of you, just as I am.'

Josée took his hand impulsively.

'Forgive me. I'm in such a muddle . . . I really don't know where I am. Tell me, Séverin, what do you think . . . is it my fault?'

He did not ask 'what?' but shook his head.

'It's not your fault, as you put it. This kind of thing is never anyone's fault. But if you mean, does it depend on you, perhaps, to put everything right, I don't think it does either. He almost took me in at first, with his ingenuous manner. If he hadn't got Laura into such a state . . .'

'What state?'

'Making her madly in love with him, seeing her every day, dazzling her and never so much as touching her . . . For God's sake, she's living on sleeping pills and sedatives. Dort wanted to take her to Egypt with him, but your husband looked desperate and said: "What shall I do without you? What about my show?" She didn't go.'

'I didn't know.'

'You don't know anything. You're so scared of getting mixed up in things that you sit dreaming of something else. Of what else, anyway?'

She began to laugh.

'Of a deserted beach.'

'Naturally. As soon as you get tired of an affair or feel

you've made a mistake, you start dreaming about deserted beaches. Do you remember . . . ?'

To his amusement, she instinctively glanced sideways.

'Don't worry, he's not here.'

'This isn't just an affair, Séverin. He's my husband, he loves me and I care about him.'

'Now don't be conventional. You got married to this one. And not to the others. So what? Don't run away, I adore it when you're angry.'

He followed her down the street, she walked ahead of him, muttering over and over again between her teeth: 'I'm not like that, I'm not like that,' until he finally grasped what she was saying.

'Of course you aren't like that. You were made for a gay, happy life and to love someone who doesn't hang on to you by the throat all the time. Are you angry with me, Josée?'

As they reached the gallery, she turned and said 'No' shortly, with her eyes full of tears. Séverin stood at the door, gaping.

Josée pushed her way through the crowd, biting her lips to check her tears. She was looking for Alan. 'Alan, my darling, you who love me too much, you who are crazy, you who aren't like the others, Alan, tell me they're wrong, that they don't understand anything about it, that it'll last for ever.' She almost ran into him as he shook hands with the last guest.

'Where were you?'

'I went to have a beer with Séverin. It was stifling here.'

'With Séverin, that's funny. I saw him here five minutes ago.'

'That's impossible. Please, don't begin all that again.'

He glanced at her and began laughing.

'You're right. This is a great day. Let's forget our little manias. Make way for painting. Make way for genius.'

She was alone with him now. The gallery was empty.

Laura motioned to them from her car. Alan took Josée by the arm and stood her before one of his pictures.

'See that? It's completely worthless. It's not painting. It's a little obsession carried out in colour. The astute critics weren't taken in let me tell you. It's a bad painting.'

'What makes you say that?'

'Because it's true. I've known all along. What do you suppose? That I've been taken in by my own make-believe? Don't you know me better?'

'Why?'

She was horror-stricken.

'To amuse myself. And to keep you busy, darling. However, I'm sorry it isn't true. You were wonderful as the painter's wife, especially the last few weeks. Reassuring ... not wildly enthusiastic about my work, no. But concealing your feelings wonderfully. It was something to keep me occupied, that was the main thing, wasn't it?'

She had recovered her self-possession and looked at him with interest.

'Why are you telling me all this now?'

'I don't feel like spending the rest of my life smearing canvas with obsessive painting. And then, I don't like lying to you,' he added gracefully.

She stood before him, motionless, confusedly remembering the sleepless nights he had made her spend, his bouts of terror, his insistence. She laughed dryly.

'You've overacted your part a little. Come, your patron is waiting for you.'

Laura was crimson with excitement and happiness. She settled herself between them in the car and talked ceaselessly. From time to time, her hand hovered rapturously, timidly, over Alan's. He responded with spontaneous gaiety, and Josée, hearing their laugher, watching the convulsive movements of Laura's hand, wished she were dead.

*

Laura's flat in the rue de Longchamp was too large, too solemn, one piece of Boule following another with the result that no one – at least when a party began – knew where to put down his glass. Josée charged through the apartment and locked herself into a bathroom where she carefully repaired the ravages caused by her brief and burning tears an hour earlier. Staring at herself in a mirror, she thought her haggard, feverish expression most becoming and gradually lengthened the curve of her eyelids, the oval of her face, filling out the line of her lower lip and finished up by smiling back at the features of an older, dangerous looking stranger that she had superimposed on her own. She felt herself growing more feverish, but not unpleasantly so, and there rose inside her a desire to destroy, to shock, that she had not felt since Key Largo. 'They're getting on my nerves,' she murmured, 'they're really beginning to get on my nerves,' and 'they' stood for an ill-defined and hypocritical multitude. She left the bathroom in high spirits, or rather, filled with a gentle rage she could no longer control. In the drawing-room, Laura and Alan leaned against a wall, holding forth gaily. A few stragglers from the exhibition had already arrived. Deliberately ignoring them, Josée helped herself to a stiff whisky from a tray. Alan called out to her.

'I thought you hadn't been drinking anything but water for the last two months!'

'I'm thirsty,' she answered, and grinned in a way that puzzled him. 'I'm drinking to your success,' she continued, raising her glass, 'and to Laura's, since it's thanks to her that everything went off so well.'

Laura smiled back at her absently and plucked at Alan's arm to attract his attention. He hesitated a second and continued staring at Josée, who gave him a big wink and turned her back on him. She glanced round the drawing-room in search of a prey, any good-looking, placid man would do so long as he took an interest in her. But the room was still almost empty. Having nothing better to do, she went and sat by Elizabeth G. who, more pallid than ever, was waiting once more for her terrifying lover. She had attempted suicide again ten days before and her wrists were bound up with greyish bandages.

'How are you?' asked Josée.

She swallowed a mouthful of whisky and thought it disgusting.

'Better, thank you.' (Elizabeth's attempts at suicide were a topic of conversation, like other people's colds.) 'I don't know what's become of Enrico, he should be here. I'm so glad about Alan, you know . . .'

'Thanks,' said Josée.

She looked at Elizabeth with an affection that would have melted the heart of a tiger.

Elizabeth warmed to such a friendly glance. After hesitating a moment, she said:

'If Enrico could only have half that much success! It would reconcile him with life, he'd be saved. For he's not on speaking terms with the rest of the world, you know.'

She announced this much as she might have mentioned a tiff between two parlourmaids. Josée nodded gravely. She felt marvellously well. Why? 'Because at last I'm living, play acting, solely for myself, without bothering any longer about that little humbug's reactions, that little humbug busy telling a few more lies over there,' and filled with savage joy, she listened to Elizabeth who continued:

'He says: "You have very devoted friends, and if only they helped me . . ." That's true, of course, but I can't force Laura to do something for him. He thinks my friends are angry with him because I complain about him. But I never complain about him. I know him. He's very talented. He's tortured by a sense of failure, by the blindness of a public that only likes secondhand work . . . er . . . I'm not talking about Alan, naturally.'

'You can,' said Josée coldly. 'I don't care for his painting, personally.'

'You're wrong there,' said Elizabeth feebly, although greatly surprised, 'there's something about it . . .'

Her bandaged wrist described a curve. Josée smiled.

'Something new, is that it? Maybe you're right. Anyway, Elizabeth, you're not to try suicide any more.'

'I must be tight,' she thought as she walked away, 'tight on two sips of whisky, it's incredible.' Someone caught her by the arm, it was Séverin.

'I want to apologize for what happened a moment ago, Josée. Did I upset you?'

He looked penitent and spoke in a gentle whisper as though to avoid wounding her further. She shook her head.

'You've broken my heart, Séverin, but cleared my brain. Do you remember that film with Bette Davis? Just as she was giving a big party at Hollywood, she heard that someone had swiped her lover.'

'*All about Eve*,' he replied, surprised.

'Yes. She went up to her guests and said: " Hold tight, things are going to hum." My dear Séverin, things are going to hum.'

'Laura? Alan?'

'No. Me.'

'Why are you made up like a vamp? Josée . . .'

He caught up with her at the bar. She very carefully slipped two ice cubes into her glass.

'What are you going to do?'

He was divided between amusement and fear. Josée's awakenings, as he called them, were often calamitous.

'I'm going to have a good time, my dear Séverin. I'm bored by the role of nurse, boy scout, and sinner all rolled into one. I'm going to have a good time. And right here, which isn't going to be any too easy. I feel so well that my wrists ache.'

'You must be careful,' said Séverin, 'don't get worked up about . . .'

But he stopped short. A man had just entered the room, smiling, affable, and Josée turned as she noticed Séverin's expression.

'This can only be one of Laura's bright ideas,' he said.

'It's dear old Marc,' said Josée quietly, and went up to him.

He had not changed: the same slightly too regular features, rather irritatingly easy manner and unfailing social good humour. He put on a theatrical expression of alarm on seeing Josée, then clasped her in his arms.

'A ghost . . . Do you still want to ruin my life? Hello, Séverin.'

'Where have you sprung from?' asked the latter gloomily.

'From Ceylon. I was there a month and a half for my paper. Before that I spent two months in New York and six weeks in London. And who do I see on my return? Josée. God bless old Laura for inviting me. What have you been doing for the last two years, my darling?'

'I've married. And in case you don't know it, this party is being given to celebrate my husband's début as a painter.'

'Married! You're crazy! Now let's see, if I've got it right – ' he drew a card from his pocket – 'you're called Mrs Ash?'

'Exactly.'

She laughed. He had not changed. In the old days he used to spend his time playing the cynical, harassed reporter and his nights telling her about the masterpiece he intended to put on the stage later.

'Mrs Ash . . . You've become even prettier. Let's have a drink together. Drop your painter and marry me.'

'I'll leave you to yourselves,' said Séverin, 'you won't need me with all your memories.'

They spent the next hour asking: 'Do you remember the day . . .?' and: 'Tell me, what's become of . . .?' etc. Josée never thought that this period of her life could have left so many memories or, above all, that she would recall them with such pleasure. She had forgotten Alan. He went past them, threw her a 'Having a good time?' and a suspiciously blank glance at Marc.

'Is that your husband?' he asked. 'He's not bad looking – and gifted too.'

'And loaded with money,' said Josée laughing.

'And he has you! It's too much,' declared Marc. 'Are you happy?'

She smiled without answering. Fortunately, Marc never dwelt on a question. His vitality was such that he continually glided from one subject to another, from one attitude to another, and this had gradually turned him into the most inconsistent and most agreeable young man in Paris. Josée remembered how sick she was of him at the end of their brief liaison and almost wondered why she felt so happy now to be with him.

'Josée,' called Laura, 'come here a moment.'

She got up, felt the floor give slightly under her feet and smiled. Laura held Alan by one arm and a stranger by the other.

'I hate to tear you away from Marc,' she said, and Alan grew pale, 'but Jean Perdet wants so much to meet you.'

She found herself exchanging a few commonplaces about painting with Perdet, who clearly wanted to meet but not to talk to her. Finally, she got rid of him and Alan joined her at once.

'So that's Marc?'

He was mumbling and must have been drinking a great

deal. His eyelids twitched. She stared at him and felt like laughing in his face.

'Yes, that's Marc.'

'He looks like a tailor's dummy.'

'He always did.'

'You were reminiscing?'

'Of course. You know what, don't you?'

'I'm delighted to think you're celebrating my success in this way.'

'Come, come! You remember what you told me?'

Thanks to the flattery and the drinks, he had probably rather forgotten about it. And in the end, the chances were that he would go on painting. She turned her back on him. The party was becoming unreal. 'He can do as he likes, as far as I'm concerned,' she thought, 'smear paint on canvas without believing in it, drive Laura to suicide.' And she went off to put some powder on.

The bathroom was occupied and she decided to use Laura's, which was a little farther away. She crossed a room hung with blue satin, where a couple of Pekinese were sleeping on the bed, and entered the tiny blue and gold bathroom. It was there that Laura probably tried to refurbish her looks in order to fascinate Alan. The idea made her smile. In the mirror, her eyes seemed dilated and lighter than usual. She leaned her brow against the glass for a moment.

'Thinking?'

Marc's voice made her start. He was leaning in the doorway in the casual attitude sometimes taken by models in *Adam*. She turned, and they smiled at each other. A single step brought him close to her. He kissed her, she struggled faintly and he released her.

'That was to remind you of the good old days,' he said a little hoarsely.

'I want him,' she thought, 'he's a little ridiculous, he

talks like a cheap novelette and I want him.' He locked the door silently and took her into his arms again. They struggled for a moment to undress one another and slipped awkwardly to the floor. He knocked himself against the bath and swore. A tap had been left running and Josée vaguely thought of getting up to turn it off, but he had already taken her hand and pressed it against his body and she remembered how proud he had always been of his virility. Nevertheless, he made love as hastily as ever, and not for an instant did Josée forget the sound of water running into the basin. Afterwards he lay prostrate on her, breathing heavily, and the cramped surroundings, the risk, the murmur of voices from the drawing-room, in retrospect, conjured up a good deal more emotion in Josée's memory than the embrace itself.

'Get up,' she said. 'They'll be looking for us. If Laura . . .' He rose, held out his hand and helped her to her feet. Her legs shook and she wondered if it were not from fright. They tidied their hair in silence.

'Can I ring you up?' he asked.

'Of course, ask Séverin.'

They looked at one another in the mirror. He seemed delighted with himself. She gave a little laugh, kissed his cheek and went out first. She knew that behind her he would be lighting a cigarette, giving his hair a final pat and would walk out at last looking so thoroughly unconcerned that the least attentive observer would have become suspicious. But who would imagine that on the very day of her young and handsome husband's exhibition, Josée Ash would make love half-dressed in a bathroom five yards square with an old friend that she was not in love with? That she had never loved? Even Alan would not think of it.

She returned to the drawing-room, drank some fruit juice and yawned discreetly. She felt sleepy, as she always did. As she always did when love was reduced to a physical act bereft of any poetry. Laura fluttered from group to group, weaving a magic circle round Alan who, gloomy and dishevelled, stood facing the gaily chattering Jean Perdet. Josée moved towards Alan, but Laura reached him first.

'The hero of the party is in a fine state! My dear Alan, you look like a thug.'

She straightened his tie, and he allowed her to do it without looking at her. Josée then realized that he was dead drunk. Laura raised her hand to smooth back his ruffled hair, and suddenly Alan tore himself away from her.

'No! You've pawed me enough for today.'

There was a terrible silence. Laura stood rooted to the spot, thunderstruck, and attempted to give a little laugh that stopped short. Alan looked down sullenly. Josée could feel herself move up to him.

'I think it's time we went home.'

The humour of her remark only struck her in the taxi. Alan had opened the window, the wind blew her hair about and at the same time revived her.

'You didn't behave very nicely,' she said.

'It's no reason because I've flirted with her once or twice for her to . . .'

The rest of the sentence died away incoherently.

Josée turned to him incredulously.

'You've flirted with her? When?'

'In the studio. The woman worked herself up to such a pitch that it finally got me going.'

'One never really knows anything about anyone,' thought Josée. 'So Alan has been moved by Laura, has sometimes fondled her out of nervous irritation or out of cruelty – does even he know which?' She asked him.

'Both,' he answered. 'She would close her eyes, sigh, and I'd stop immediately, apologize, talk about you, about her husband, about her great soul and about me, the great painter. Josée, when will we extricate ourselves from all these lies, I'm stifling, when shall we leave for Key Largo?'

'You're responsible for the lies,' she said. 'You and you alone. You're too fond of them.'

She spoke sadly, gently. The taxi tore through the grey streets; the trees shone under the lights.

'What about that Marc?'

'Nothing.'

She answered curtly, and for once he was not insistent.

*

Marc telephoned the next morning at eleven sharp, at a lucky moment when Alan was having a shower. So Josée was able to make an appointment for that afternoon, at a time when she knew that Alan would be busy with the manager of the picture gallery and several photographers. She felt no pleasure whatever in arranging their meeting, but simply a desire to sink into something, to destroy an idea of herself that she had harboured too long. After which Alan came out of the bathroom and rang up Laura. He calmly informed her that his outburst of the evening before had been inevitable and that he imagined that she must have understood it perfectly. There was an astounded silence at the other end of the line, and Josée, who was dressing, paused, motionless.

'Josée suspects that our relations have gone beyond the limits of mere friendship,' continued Alan, smiling at his wife. 'She's adorable, of course, but morbidly jealous. I wanted to reassure her by reversing our roles and leading her to believe that it was you who . . . well, who had a weakness for me.'

Seated on the edge of the bed, wrapped in a red bathrobe, he never took his eyes off her. She stood before him, bewildered. He handed her the second receiver and she took it mechanically.

'I suspected it,' replied Laura's voice – faltering but infinitely relieved. 'Alan, my dear, no one must know of our mutual affinity. We haven't the right to make others suffer and . . .'

Josée tossed her receiver on to the bed. She felt ashamed, and with a sort of horror watched Alan as he continued talking in the same tender, considerate tone. After persuading Laura to meet him at the gallery during the afternoon, he hung up.

'Well played!' he cried. 'Did you see how I turned the tables?'

'I really don't see where all this is getting you,' observed Josée, controlling her voice.

'Nowhere. Why should you want it to get me anywhere? That's the great difference between us, darling. When you marry, it's to have children, when you talk to a man, it's to go to bed with him. I make love to a woman I don't want and paint without believing in my work. That's all.'

He ceased joking suddenly and came closer to her.

'In this gigantic farce that is the sum of human life, I don't see why I shouldn't have my own little jokes. What are you going to do while I'm discussing painting with my girl friend?'

'Make love with Marc,' she replied gaily.

'You'd better be careful, I'm still having you followed,' he said, and laughed too.

There was a strange ache in her heart as she remembered their first walk together in Central Park, how painstakingly she had attempted to understand him, what an immense amount of tenderness, interest, and sweetness she had advanced, like everybody else who begins to love someone.

They lunched on oysters and various cheeses in a sumptuous *bistro* – Alan could not bear anything but white tablecloths – and parted at two-thirty. 'I'm being followed,' thought Josée, and walked slowly to avoid tiring the private eye. Maybe he was old and shabby and sick of his profession, maybe he even entertained a vague affection for her after three months . . . Did such things ever happen? In any case, she was leading him straight to the café where Marc was waiting for her. He greeted her with shrieks of joy and she looked at him in amazement. What mental aberration could have made her think him amusing the evening before? He held forth, he smelt of lavender, he said hello to everyone. But a single reason had brought her there – or rather, a single unreason, for, even on that score, she preferred Alan a thousand times over. She smiled significantly at him once or twice and he got up, immediately.

'Do you want to . . .?'

She nodded. Yes, she wanted to. But wanted what? A little amusement, put Alan in the right, vaguely destroy herself? He took her away with him at once. They climbed into a small, back-firing car, of the kind reporters love, and to frighten her, he took two or three pretty sharp turns. In spite of his fatuousness, he seemed a trifle perplexed.

Things took place just as they had the evening before, although more comfortably, thanks to a conspicuously large bed that took up a great deal of room in Marc's studio. Afterwards, he lit a cigarette, handed it to her, and began his questions:

'Tell me about your husband? You don't love him? Or isn't he very skilful? They say that Americans . . .'

'Don't pry,' said Josée dryly.

'I really can't believe you're in love with me, can I?'

The 'can I' was a masterpiece of intonation. Josée smiled, stretched, stubbed out her cigarette in an ashtray.

'No,' she replied. 'Not at all. I'm destroying things at the moment. I'm even destroying something that used to mean a lot to me.'

She felt sorry for herself.

'Why?' he asked.

Nevertheless, he seemed a little annoyed by the evident sincerity of her 'no'.

'It comes to this: it's either that or me.'

'Will he find out about it?'

'He pays a man who is waiting for me downstairs. A private detective.'

'Not really?'

The idea delighted him. He bounded to the window, saw no one and put on a fierce expression to amuse her, then looked panicky and suddenly took her in his arms when she began to laugh.

'I adore it when you laugh.'

'Did I laugh much, before?'

'Before what?'

She almost answered 'before Alan' but refrained.

'Before I went to New York.'

'Yes, very often. You were very gay.'

'I was twenty-two, when I first knew you, wasn't I?'

'Just about. Why?'

'I'm twenty-seven now. That alters things. I don't laugh so much these days. And then I used to drink to get closer to people, and now I drink to forget them. Funny, isn't it?'

'It doesn't sound it,' he muttered.

She ran her hand over Marc's cheek. He lived his little life, between his reporting and his studio and his easy feminine conquests. He was kind and talkative, he was a pleasant specimen of humanity. He was straightforward, boring, and a bit smug. She sighed.

'I must go home.'

'If you're really being followed, what's going to happen?'

He smiled as he said this, and she frowned.

'You don't believe me?'

'No. You always had the wildest stories to tell. I adored

it. Everybody adored it. Especially because you obviously didn't believe in them yourself.'

'I suppose in those days,' she said, 'I was gay and rather crazy.'

'You still are,' he began, then stopped.

They looked at each other, and for the first time Marc wondered if some of the implications of the situation had escaped him. This put him in a bad temper and he drove her home at top speed. At her door, he hesitated.

'Tomorrow?'

'I'll ring you up at your office.'

She walked slowly up the stairs. It was seven o'clock. By this time, Alan must know that she had gone into a house on the rue des Petits-Champs at three-thirty and had only left the place two hours later. Her hands trembled as she looked for her key, but she knew that she must go in, that it was the only solution.

He was there, sure enough, lying on the sofa, holding an evening paper. He smiled and stretched out his hand towards her. She sat down by him.

'Things are going very badly in the Congo, you know. A plane has crashed near Brussels. The papers are quite funereal, these days.'

'Did you see Laura?'

She was desperately enjoying these last moments of peace when she could still talk to him as a friend, even if he was shaking with rage inside.

'Of course I saw Laura. She's behaving like a conspirator.'

He seemed very gay. She hesitated for a second.

'And you've had your report?'

'My report?'

'From the private detective who follows me around.'

He burst out laughing.

'The idea! That didn't last two weeks. If you had the

least inclination for anyone, our good friends would have informed me of it.'

All of a sudden, she sank down and stretched out beside him, her head on his shoulder. A feeling of great gentleness came over her. She still had the choice, but knew that it had already been taken, that the tears she had shed in New York on Bernard's shoulder, in an air-conditioned bar, as she thought of Alan, of herself, of their joint failure, corresponded to a deep truth. Deeper than the habit she had of the tranquil body next her and of the shielding arm on which her head was resting. Their story had died that day on the very instant when she realized that she could not tell it to Bernard or even to herself. The truth about her marriage was both too subtle and too passionate, it resided in moments of tenderness, of pleasure and of cruelty. It was neither a dialogue nor a partnership. She sighed. Alan's hand stroked her hair tenderly.

Her eyes wandered over the dark beams, the light walls, the few pictures in the room. 'How long have I lived here? Five months, six?' She closed her eyes. 'And with this man breathing so quietly by my side, two years and a half, three? What shall I do, where shall I go and who with?' All these questions seemed urgent to her, yet absurd, each one of them depended on the little sentence that she must first say, and that her whole body, every muscle in her face refused to utter. 'I must wait,' she thought, 'wait and talk of something else, take a deep breath and then I'll be able to say it easily, at one go.'

'Tell me something about Marc,' said Alan's mocking voice as he took his hand from Josée's hair.

'I spent the afternoon with him at his flat.'

'I'm not joking,' he said.

'Nor am I.'

There was a short silence. Then Josée began to speak. She told him everything in the greatest detail: what the apartment was like, how he had undressed her, their positions, their caresses, what he had said when he took her, a particular demand of his afterwards. She used the most precise terms, made a real effort to remember everything. Alan remained motionless. When she had finished, he gave a strange sigh.

'Why are you telling me all this?'

'So that you don't have to ask me.'

'You'll do it again?'

'Yes.'

It was true, and he must have realized it. She turned her head towards him. He did not seem to be suffering; he looked disappointed and this confirmed what Josée had thought.

'Have I left anything out?'

'No,' he replied slowly. 'I think you've said everything, everything of interest to me. Everything I might have imagined,' he shouted abruptly. He sat up and, for the first time, looked at her with hatred.

She looked at him steadily, and he went down suddenly on his knees, his head against her, shaken with dry sobs.

'What have I done?' he whispered. 'What have I done to you? – what have we done?'

She neither moved nor answered. She listened to a great emptiness settling within her.

'I wanted all of you,' he went on, 'I wanted the worst.'

'I couldn't keep it up,' she said simply, and he raised his head.

He made a last attempt:

'It was a mistake.'

But he did not mean her day with Marc, he meant her description and she knew it.

'It would always be like that,' she said gently, 'the game is over.'

For a long time they remained as they were, close to one another like two wrestlers, exhausted.

More about Penguins

Penguin Book News, an attractively illustrated magazine
which appears every month, contains details of all
the new books issued by Penguins as they are published.
Every four months it is supplemented by
Penguins in Print, which is a complete list of all books
published by Penguins which are still available.
(There are well over two thousand of these.)

A specimen copy of *Penguin Book News* can be sent to
you free on request, and you can become a regular
subscriber at 3s. for one year (with the complete lists).
Just write to Dept EP, Penguin Books Ltd,
Harmondsworth, Middlesex, enclosing a cheque or
postal order, and your name will be added to the
mailing list.

Other volumes of Françoise Sagan published by
Penguins are described overleaf.

Note: *Penguin Book News* and *Penguins in Print*
are not available in the U.S.A. or Canada

OTHER PENGUINS BY FRANÇOISE SAGAN

BONJOUR TRISTESSE

Bonjour Tristesse describes the indignation of a young girl at her father's plan to remarry.

'The virtuosity is dazzling throughout ... She is marvellously gifted' – *Sunday Times*

A CERTAIN SMILE

The dilemma of a young girl when she falls out of love with her student friend and into an entanglement with his uncle.

'Some of the writing can without exaggeration be compared with Stendhal' – *The Times Literary Supplement*

AIMEZ-VOUS BRAHMS

At thirty-nine a Parisian career girl is torn between the champagne of youth and the security of age.

'Easily her best' – *Guardian*

THOSE WITHOUT SHADOWS

A vivid picture of a group of artists and intellectuals trapped in an aimless dissatisfaction that seems to envelop Paris.

'Memorable with simplicity that deceives and immense precision of phrase ... full of laughter, never bitter' – *Daily Telegraph*

NOT FOR SALE IN THE U.S.A. OR CANADA